The Super-secret diary of HOLLY HOPKINSON

This is going to be a fiasco!

CHARLIE P. BROOKS
and KATY RIDDELL

HarperCollins *Children's Books*

First published in Great Britain by
HarperCollins *Children's Books* in 2021
HarperCollins *Children's Books* is a division of HarperCollins*Publishers* Ltd,
1 London Bridge Street
London SE1 9GF

www.harpercollins.co.uk

HarperCollins*Publishers*
1st Floor, Watermarque Building
Ringsend Road
Dublin 4, Ireland

1

HB ISBN 978-0-00-832808-5
PB ISBN 978-0-00-832811-5

Charlie Brooks and Katy Riddell assert the moral right to be
identified as the author and illustrator of the work respectively.

A CIP catalogue record for this title is available from the British Library.

Printed and bound in Great Britain by CPI Group (UK) Ltd, Croydon, CR04YY

MIX
Paper from
responsible sources
FSC™ C007454

This book is produced from independently certified FSC™ paper
to ensure responsible forest management.

For more information visit: www.harpercollins.co.uk/green

For Big Bean and Little Bean

CHARACTERS

HOLLY
HOPKINSON

◁ VINNIE

DAD

◁ AUNT
ELECTRA

HAROLD

MUM

HARMONY

DAFFODIL

GRANDPA

THIS IS ME

PROLOGUE

THESE ARE THE *LIVE* MEMOIRS OF
HOLLY HOPKINSON, WHO IS NEARLY TEN.

I am writing them by my own fair hand so that
historians and people from all over the world
will have a real-life account of what life was like
in twenty-first-century London without all the
usual rubbish that adults put in.

Who knows how far in the future it will be
before *you* get to read them, dear reader. I imagine
it could be hundreds – even squillions – of years
before they are dug up,

⭐ published to international bestselling acclaim,

⭐ set behind glass at the British Museum,

⭐ studied in schools across the country

and

☆ turned into a Hollywood movie . . .

★ THE SUPER SECRET DIARY OF HOLLY HOPKINSON: THE MOVIE ★

If Hollywood still exists!

My family, THE HOPKINSONS, live in a lovely, warm, clean, modern house, thank you very much. My dad has a job in an office. I have *no* idea what he does, but he always wears a suit.

Mum works in PR. When I ask her what that is, she says it's

'TAKING MONEY OFF IDIOTS WHO HAVE NO IMAGINATION'.

Harmony Hopkinson, my elder sister, is going through a difficult stage – well, that's what I heard Mum saying to her teacher in her *serious* voice.

Harmony treats me like a little sister a bit *too* much. She needs to think more about how she's going to look when these memoirs are published.

She's only happy when she's going off to demonstrate* about something she disapproves of.

Harold Hopkinson is my older brother. He's a bit stroppy and talks a load of codswallop. *And* he gets double-whopper spots on his nose these days. Dad says *he* was like Harold when he was younger, and Mum just says,

'NOW, WHY DOESN'T THAT SURPRISE ME?'

But I really don't know why Dad says he *was* like Harold, because he flipping well still *is*.

 We also have a dog called Barkley, who likes eating and going to the park.

He also thinks the poodle who we sometimes bump into is the bee's knees. If he doesn't tone down his BOGGLE-EYES stuff we're going to get into *serious* trouble with the authorities.

* DEMONSTRATE –
to shout and scream
like the devil.

Finally, there's Aunt Electra, who lives in Hackney and visits us all the time.

'ECCENTRIC' →
SAYS DAD

'ANNOYING'
SAYS MUM →

'THE GREATEST' →
SAYS ME

'SMELLS OF →
CANDYFLOSS'
SAYS ME

AUNT ELECTRA

Despite our fab house and the corner shop at the end of our cul-de-sac, which stocks everything we need, Mum wants to move to a different area. (Dad says she's 'upwardly mobile'. I think it's caused by her PILATES classes.)

But we'll see about that – the rest of our family are quite happy being *im*mobile, thank you very much.

4

I *quite* like my school, in spite of the teachers who are a SHAMBLES. At least they don't bother much about homework, and if I sit at the back of the classroom, I can talk as much as I like to my *best* friend in the world, Aleeshaa.

We are inseparable.

And Aleeshaa always has loads of pocket money, so after PE we'll gallivant across the park to the corner shop to buy stuff.

Once a week I'm allowed to go to Aleeshaa's house for tea. They live in a very swish flat above her father's art gallery up on Notting Hill.

Dad's always been a bit funny about Aleeshaa's father since they met at what Mum calls 'ONE OF THOSE PAINFUL PARENTS' EVENINGS'.

'Anyone would think he invented art,' Dad said.

'Excuse you, Dad,' I said in my *unforgiving* voice. 'Aleeshaa's father knows a lot about art . . . and so does Aleeshaa . . . she's going to art school, and she's got a mobile phone.'

'Fancy that,' Dad replied, pulling one of his goofy faces to Mum. 'But I can't quite make the connection between—'

'ENOUGH, GEORGE,'

said Mum. 'And you would still have a phone, Holly, if you hadn't dropped your old one down the loo.'

Thanks for the reminder I don't need, Mum.

R.I.P

6

Anyway,
Aleeshaa and I have an

UNBREAKABLE BOND,

whatever my dad thinks. She says I should go
to art school with her, so I'm probably going to
do that.

Yes. All in all, my life is pretty

BOB'S-YOUR-UNCLE great.

Or so I thought.

CHAPTER 1
THE WHIFF OF BAD NEWS

OFFICIAL BREAKING NEWS:
IT ALL STARTED TO GO **WRONG** TODAY.

When I woke up this morning, I was very, very happy. Probably even happier than the queen; unless she had something special planned for breakfast.

Mum was flitting* around the kitchen looking like a packet of vacuum-packed bacon. She was going to a dance class on her way to work.

'Holly, your turn to take Barkley out,' she shouted as her Lycra-clad bottom disappeared out of the door.

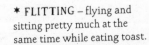

> * FLITTING – flying and sitting pretty much at the same time while eating toast.

8

The poodle doesn't get up very early, so at least we wouldn't have any bother on that front.

Dad left late for work, as usual. He says,

'IT DOESN'T MATTER BECAUSE EVERYONE WHO WORKS IN MY OFFICE IS A MORON,'

when he is running late – well, more like *walking* late, really.

Harold was the least happy person in our family this morning. The neighbours complained (again!) to the coppers about his drumming, and now his drum kit is about to be the subject of a court order.

Which will be a setback to his career as a platinum-record-selling, stadium-filling ROCKSTAR.

Harmony was being fine *for her* – she's planning a DEMONSTRATION outside someone's embassy on social media, with some new friends who she's never met.

I tried to get some intel on what she's up to, but she won't tell me, as per usual. Harmony likes to support a lot of causes in her spare time – particularly when the weather's nice.

o o o

School was quiet today, and then Aleeshaa and I went to 'after-school coding camp'; which is secret code for eating sweets and listening to music on Aleeshaa's phone because the teacher didn't turn up, as usual.

When I got home, I could tell all was not well. The air was hanging heavy with the

whiff of *bad* news.

Dad was on *his* phone to Aunt Electra in one room.

I heard him say,

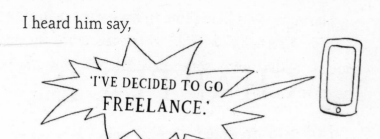

'I'VE DECIDED TO GO FREELANCE.'

But Mum was on *her* phone in the kitchen to one of her book-club friends. She said, 'He's been fired . . . can't say I'm surprised.' But this is the weird bit. Mum then said,

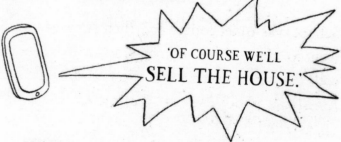

'OF COURSE WE'LL SELL THE HOUSE.'

What I can't work out is how Dad going freelance means that Mum can finally make us all mobile upwards?

IT JUST DOESN'T MAKE SENSE.

CHAPTER 2
THE GRIM REALITY

THE **BAD NEWS** IS THAT WE ARE DOWNWARDLY - NOT UPWARDLY - MOBILE.

And we're not just moving down a little bit; if life is a game of Snakes and Ladders, we have just flipping well landed on a jumbo PYTHON.

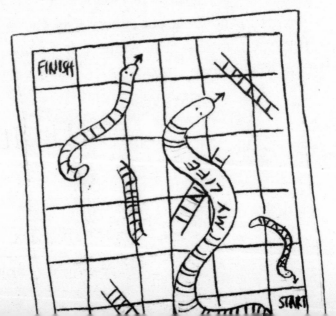

We are moving out to the countryside, to live on a farm with our grandpa near Chipping Topley.

TOMORROW.

I rang Aleeshaa straight away to tell her the horrible news, and all she said was,

'HEY ... THAT'S RANDOM.'

Erm, it's a bit more than random, bestie.

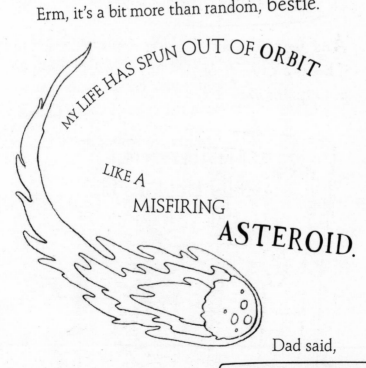

MY LIFE HAS SPUN OUT OF ORBIT LIKE A MISFIRING ASTEROID.

Dad said,

'IT WON'T BE FOREVER.'

13

But Mum made an expression like she'd sat on a very cold loo seat when he said that, so it will probably be for *ages*.

I pointed out to Dad that Dick Whittington didn't bolt for the hills when he lost his job and went freelance.

But Dad just said,

'WELL,
DICK WHITTINGTON ONLY
HAD A CAT TO FEED.'

So the Hopkinson family are being sentenced to a life of poverty, manure and FERAL people who speak funny – because of the price of CAT FOOD?

LET HISTORY RECORD:

I, Holly Hopkinson,
am NOT happy.

CHAPTER 3
THE LONG MARCH

I WAS UP SPIT-SPOT BRIGHT AND EARLY
TO TAKE BARKLEY OUT TO THE PARK FOR
ONE LAST TIME. THE POOR, UNSUSPECTING
BRUTE MIGHT NEVER SEE ONE AGAIN.

Then I popped round to Aleeshaa's swish flat to say goodbye – maybe *forever*? I asked her if she wanted to come and wave us off, but she said she had to help in her dad's gallery today.

She seems to be getting over my bombshell **DEPARTURE NEWS** quite well; too well, in fact. I mean, it wouldn't have hurt her to do a bit of desperate wailing, would it?

Anyway, when I got home there was still masses of our junk to load up.

What was clear was that we were not going to get all of our stuff in the lorry. So Dad said he was making an 'executive decision' about what we had to leave behind.

Harold's drum kit made it on to the lorry, of course. But my Wendy house did not. I put up quite a stink, but Dad said I haven't used it for years and we all have to make SACRIFICES. So I said,

'FINE, I'LL SACRIFICE HAROLD.'

None of our neighbours came to wave us off – not even the ones who called the coppers about the drumming. And to make matters worse, when we drove off down the road, guess what crossed in front of the lorry?

YES.

A flipping BLACK CAT, thank you very much.

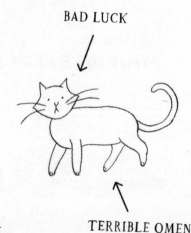

BAD LUCK

TERRIBLE OMEN

Several hours later, we are a very demoralised bunch as we head 'out into the sticks', as Mum calls it. Dad says he's felt better. Mum has certainly looked better. And I am very nervous and DOWNCAST.

Harmony has decided to wear BLACK for our pilgrimage.

Sulky Harold, of course, is the winner here. Even he can work out that he and his drum kit are wriggling from the grasp of the LAW by doing a sunlight flit.

So these could be the last words of Holly Hopkinson, if I disappear from the face of the Earth and my literary legacy is tragically cut short.

AU REVOIR, LONDON – UNTIL I RETURN AS LORD MAYOR.

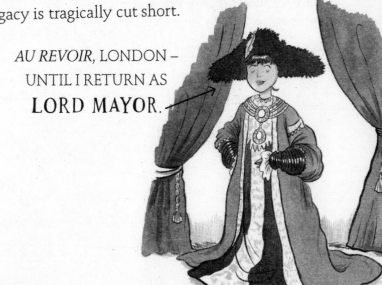

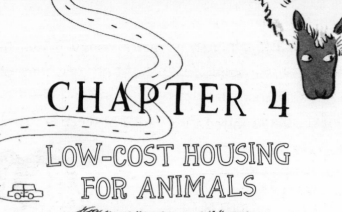

CHAPTER 4
LOW-COST HOUSING
FOR ANIMALS

JOURNEY NEWS:

THERE'S A SERVICE STATION ON THE WAY
TO CHIPPING TOPLEY, SO WE STOPPED TO
GET SOMETHING TO EAT THERE. MUM HAD
USED MOVING AS A REASON FOR FAILING TO
PROVIDE ANY BREAKFAST – WE CAN ADD
THAT TO HER 'EXCUSES' LIST.

Dad moaned that the service was 'terrible'. Mum
blurted out that she must have eaten a dodgy prawn
last night and she had to rush to the bogs* *very* fast.

Clearly things would have been a LOT MORE
TERRIBLE if the 'terrible service' station hadn't
been there.

* BOGS – toilets.

Dad said, 'Unlucky to get a dodgy prawn in spaghetti bolognaise,' when Mum was out of earshot.

Harmony spotted a lorry load of sheep at the 'terrible service' station.

'WE SHOULD ... LIKE ... SOOO LET THEM OUT,'

she suggested in her 'REBEL' voice.

'Why would you want to do that?' Dad asked.

'Cos, like, it's so **cruel**,' Harmony pronounced.

'And what exactly, *like*, is letting a gang of sheep loose in a service station?'

Dad always likes to say 'like' to Harmony. He thinks he's hilarious.

After we'd eaten, we set off again on our sorry voyage – hours and hours fighting our way down the motorway – well, at least **two**, anyway.

'Are we nearly there yet?' Mum asked for the squillionth time.

19

'Why are the fields full of animals?' Harold asked Dad as we got near Chipping Topley. 'Haven't they got any HOUSES to live in?'

'Well, Harold, one of the **great things** about coming to live in the countryside is that you can learn all about animals,' Dad replied.

Harold rolled his eyes grumpily.

'What's, like, another great thing?' Harmony asked unhelpfully.

'Well, err, let's see,' stammered Dad, 'ERR . . .'

'We're waiting,' said Mum, ganging up with Harmony.

'Hey . . . that's where the animals live,' Harmony shouted from the back of the car. 'See in that field . . . that's, like, **low-cost** HOUSING for animals.'

'I think you'll find that's, *like*, SOLAR PANELS, Harmony,' Dad corrected.

'They look cool anyway. The whole countryside should be covered in them,' Harmony declared.

Two minutes later the sat nav announced,

'YOU HAVE REACHED YOUR DESTINATION.'

We were at the end of a skew-whiff track in the middle of a field.

'ARE YOU KIDDING?'

asked Harmony.

'That's very strange,' said Dad. 'I'm sure I put the right postcode in.'

'Please tell me we're not lost,' Mum muttered.

'Please tell me we *are* lost,' chirped Harmony. 'Otherwise this is, like, where we're soooo going to live – *ugh* – basic.'

'You *have* been to your father's before, haven't you?' Mum asked Dad.

'It was a while ago,' he said nervously, '**and** Grandpa picked me up from the station. **And** it was dark. **And**, by the way . . . if it wasn't for you thinking that shoes only work on TARMAC, perhaps you and the kids might have been here before . . . that would have been helpful.'

'Calm down, everyone,' I said. 'Let's just ring Grandpa and ask him for directions.'

'GOOD IDEA, HOLLY,'

said Dad.

'Slight problem,' said Mum, looking at her phone.

'THERE'S NO RECEPTION.'

Dad started rubbing his forehead.

'We should protest,' cried Harmony. 'It's basic **human rights** . . . the downtrodden country folk are being silenced by the government.'

'For goodness' sake,' Dad shouted. 'Can I have some shush to think – and stop drumming on my sodding car seat, Harold, *please*.'

WE ARE REFUGEES – and this is officially the opposite of the best day of my life.

☆ **OFFICIAL NEWS QUESTION:** ☆

What is the **survival rate** of people who move from London to the Chipping Topley area?

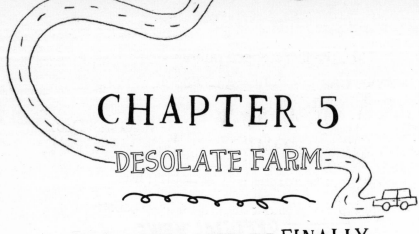

CHAPTER 5
DESOLATE FARM

HALF AN HOUR LATER WE FINALLY
FOUND THE TRACK DOWN TO GRANDPA'S
FARM, JUST OUTSIDE A VILLAGE
CALLED LOWER GORING.

'Are you sure this is right?' Mum asked.

'This sooo *can't* be right,' piped up Harmony.

'The road is just mud and there are, like, no streetlights. No one could possibly live down here.'

'Well, Grandpa does,' said Dad. 'I know where I am now.' There were exactly thirty-seven holes in the lane, and each made the car go *bonk* as Dad crawled down the track. It felt like we were in a giant carwash as the grass swept against the sides. When we *finally* drove into Grandpa's farmyard, Mum whispered, 'OH MY ...'

24

Then she just stopped talking.

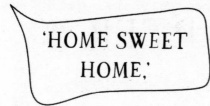

'HOME SWEET HOME,' suggested Dad.

No one else said a word for a few seconds.

'Please tell me this isn't where we're going to live,' groaned Harmony. 'Look, there's, like, poo everywhere. I am *not* getting out of the car in my new Converse.'

'Come on, everyone,' Mum said in her special voice that she uses with foreign people. 'We'd better get out.'

'Yes . . . let's go and explore,' said Dad.

You'd have thought we'd just arrived at DISNEYLAND.

Grandpa came hobbling out of a shed.

'But he's still wearing . . .' Harmony's words trailed off.

'ENOUGH!' shouted Mum.

Grandpa has got quite hairy around the facial area since last Christmas. And Harmony was right – his clothes were *precisely* the same ones he was wearing months ago, down to the egg stain on the jumper. Maybe he only owns one outfit.

VERY
PLEASED

OVERGROWN
BEARD

GRANDPA

EGG STAIN

He seemed *very* pleased to see us. Although there wasn't exactly a stampede to go and give him a hello hug.

Dad says Mum's very urban. This is *not* what she has been hoping for in life. And you can double-whopper treble that for me, thank you very much. They don't even have bins here like they do in the park in London.

○ ○ ○

For days after we arrived, Dad just walked around going,

'MARVELLOUS. SO KIND OF GRANDPA TO GIVE US HIS HOUSE.'

Yeah, about the 'house'.

I can only assume that farmers were very short when this house was built. Mum and Dad have to bend their necks to get through the door from the hall into the kitchen.

When Dad came back in from Grandpa's shed he was so cheerful he forgot to duck, so he's now got a **lump** on his head like a double-yolk egg.

But the first thing that hit me was the PONG: there is a very nasty niff in this house; a veritable not-nice **stink**.

I think it's something rotting in the wrong place, at the wrong time. And we're breathing in the PONG all the time now. A few fumes from diesel cars revving their engines at the traffic lights would be a treat, thank you *very* much.

Mum keeps going around spraying everything; including Moggy, Grandpa's ancient cat, which did not go down well with her. But it hasn't made any difference – in fact, I think it's made matters a squillion times worse.

And because the windows are tiny – probably to stop robbers climbing through them (the folk are like that in the countryside, I presume) – it's really **DARK** inside. And guess who got the worst minging bedroom, right at the end of the house down a dark, creaky corridor?

- YES. - Holly Hopkinson, of course.

The house also makes SPOOKY haunted noises at night.

The door to the attic is locked too – something **fishy** is definitely going on up there.

When I asked Grandpa about it he told me,

'THERE'S THE GHOST OF AN OLD FARMER'S WIFE CALLED MABEL UP THERE, AND SHE IS NOT VERY HAPPY.'

WHOOOOH

Apparently as long as we don't go poking around up there, goofing about and disturbing her, she'll be OK.

I've been saying a quick

GOODNIGHT, MABEL

to her every night, just to be on the safe side. I don't want to get off on the wrong foot with any GHOSTS.

There really are a lot of animals in the farmyard – most of which seem to think it's fine to come into the house whenever they jolly well feel like it, which Mum does *not* like.

There are:

☆ Chickens

☆ Ducks

EGGS

MORE EGGS, YUCK – DISGUSTING COLOUR

☆ Cow

NEEDS MILKING TWICE A DAY

☆ Pigs

JUST POO EVERYWHERE AND THEY EAT EVERYTHING

☆ Beanstalk   VERY OLD AND VERY SMALL (MORE ABOUT THAT CATASTROPHE LATER)

☆ High Five

A TITCHY FOAL

And last and least, Moggy, who, since Mum sprayed her, smells like Harold did when he tried to sort out his personal smell issue (PSI).

Mum says Moggy is like
Squirrel Nutkin:

excessively
impertinent.

Grandpa also has apple trees and gooseberry bushes. The apples don't taste anything like the ones from the shops and are mostly the wrong shape. The gooseberries are yummy, but I ate so many today I had to spend an hour on the bog that I do not wish to think about ever again.

Enough said.

Harmony keeps asking,

'WHY CAN'T WE GO TO THE SUPERMARKET TO GET OUR FOOD LIKE EVERYONE ELSE?'

But there is the faint glimmer of **GOOD NEWS** in an oasis of despair. Grandpa is actually **lovely** – much nicer than when he comes down to London for Christmas – and seems to be really excited that his family have come to live with him. Maybe he was a bit lonely before, not having anyone but his animals to talk to.

My memoirs, however, may be cruelly cut short by either a GHOST or a farmyard PLAGUE.

If that is what's meant to be, then these words will be the crumbs that my readers shall have to feast on.

I might be EXTERMINADOED.

MY LIFE IS HANGING BY
A THREAD.

CHAPTER 6

SETTLING IN . . .
AND THE **BLEAK** REALITY
OF OUR LIVES

COMMUNICATION NEWS:

I CANNOT SURVIVE IN THIS PLACE WITHOUT
A PHONE – HOW ELSE AM I GOING TO KEEP
IN TOUCH WITH ALEESHAA? DAD'S ALWAYS
ON THE LAPTOP, 'FREELANCING', AND HAROLD
AND HARMONY GUARD THEIR PHONES
WITH THEIR **TEETH**.

Mum is the lucky one. She gets to compute* from Chipping Topley back to London. Although sometimes she's going to stay over in town with one of her mates if she's got **Girls' Book Club** on.

> * COMPUTE – calculating things on a train.

36

(Dad calls it 'booze club' – and sometimes I don't think Mum even reads the actual book, judging by her Google search history.)

What happens in animal farm?

I love the train. We went to the seaside on one once. But Mum says they're not all as nice as that. She claims a man tried to pick her up in the buffet carriage the other day.

'Was the train moving?' I asked. 'If it was then that's really DANGEROUS.'

Dad is now a rural freelancer, as I mentioned earlier. It seems like a jolly nice job to me. He watches *loads* of TV when he eventually gets out of bed halfway through the morning. Which of course makes it OK for Harold to do the same, scratching and picking his nose all day.

Dad says that's his 'thinking time'.

I've noticed that Dad doesn't have to wear a suit to do freelancing in the countryside – and I think the job may have something to do with beer. When he comes back from meetings in the village, he always smells of it.

I quizzed him about that the other night when he got home and he said,

'SHUSH, YOUR MOTHER MIGHT HEAR.'

'SO?' I asked.

'Look, you can have an hour of social-media time on my laptop if you just keep quiet,' he whispered.

So we settled on an hour and a half, which meant at least I got to see what Aleeshaa was up to.

@X_ALEESHAA_X

AMAZING Concert @ hyde park

(There were a lot of photos of some concert in Hyde Park, which made me *dead* jealous.)

It's still the summer holidays, but Mum and Dad have organised what's happening with school in September. I've got a place at the primary school in Lower Goring, but Harold and Harmony are going to big school in town.

I *do not* envy them that.

We went there and it's like something out of a war documentary. Of course, I actually went to a big school in London and saw new kids arrive all the time, and it was *brutal*. What I need is a small pond that I can be a big fish in.

Naturally, Harmony is still trying to spend all her time online with her protester friends she's never met, but the Wi-Fi is not on her side,

HA HA.

Good luck organising a sit-in at the Chipping Topley abattoir when you have to stand on tiptoes and hold your phone above your head to get a signal.

Harold is making **no** effort at all to get into our new life. All he does is GRUNT at me and then go back to listening to his

thump,
thump,
thump

music with his headphones on.

But here is today's **SOCIAL NEWS** –

♡ Grandpa has what Dad is calling a

'lady friend'.

♡ ♡ ♡

'WASN'T EXPECTING THAT,'

♡

Dad said when Vera first arrived in the kitchen 'like she owns the place'. (Mum)

Officially I do not know if I like this woman – she is the BOSSY type, if you'll pardon my French.

VERA LIVES ON THE NEXT-DOOR FARM

DOES GRANDPA'S WASHING

HAS GRANDSON MY AGE CALLED VINNIE

SPEAKS A BIT FUNNY

Vera does stuff for Grandpa like his washing. She hung his pants up today on the line in the yard and there were a lot of holes in the Bottom Music area. She'd get arrested if she pulled a stunt like that in our street in London.

And that's only the **half** of it.

Vera has a grandson my age called Vinnie who came along with her today.

41

He is definitely **not** useful-new-friend material. I highly doubt that his dad owns an art gallery as swish as Aleeshaa's. And he doesn't have a smartphone I can borrow until I get mine.

I said,

'HOW DO YOU DO?'

And he replied,

'ALL RIIIGHT.'

Mum said to Dad in an adult whisper, 'Oh, look, a nice young man for Holly to get to know!' and winked.

I am FURIOUS.
ABSOLUTELY FURIOUS.

Dad said, 'I don't know, is he the FULL SHILLING?' Whatever that means.

THE FULL SHILLING

But Vinnie goes to the school I'll be going to, so I shall be sucking as much information out of him as I can and making an ally of him. After all, Alexander the Great didn't get to rule the world without allies, and Holly Hopkinson will need a few if she's going to see off the local kids at Lower Goring School and stop them submerging her with their ducking stool.

BIG-PICTURE NEWS – there IS a member of my family who can blow some life into my survival campaign . . . I'm going to officially invite Aunt Electra down for my birthday, which is coming up soon.

I will have to write her a letter as I *still* don't have a new phone.

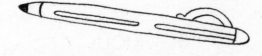

Dear Aunt Electra,

I hope you are well.

I thought you might be worrying about how things are going on the farm, so I'm writing to tell you – NOT GOOD is the answer.

It's in the middle of **nowhere**, and it is not my family's natural habitat, I can tell you.

43

Dad has become addicted to daytime TV shows,

 Mum cavorts off to London every day,

Harmony only cares about Harmony

 and Harold is a big lump of scratching, grunting doofus.

Grandpa is nice to everyone – too nice, if you ask me – particularly to this woman called Vera who seems to be pitching for squatters' rights.

Grandpa is a bit different from what I expected. To start with, he doesn't seem to do any farming at all – which is odd for a farmer. He is what Dad calls 'a dark horse'.

GRANDPA

Please will you come to my birthday party, Aunt Electra? It will be great fun and there will be **lots** of messing about.

If you don't come it will be the **worst** day of my life.

Lots of love,

Your distressed niece clinging on to humanity,

Holly..

PS As I can't text you I've had to resort to pen and ink. So if you came across a second-hand smartphone it would be a most welcome surprise birthday present. If you know the right people they're quite cheap, and I don't mind a few dents.

CHAPTER 7

NO WAY, JOSÉ

TODAY I AM IN THE DEPTHS OF *DESPAIR*.
A DARK CLOUD OF DESPONDENCY IS HANGING
OVER ME LIKE THE HANGMAN'S GUILLOTINE.

First of all, I am missing Aleeshaa.

But I think it is well documented that Dad will
not be inviting Aleeshaa's family to the farm any
time soon – ever, in fact – so my dream is slipping
away from me.

If it's OK for Mum to compute to London every day, I can see no reason why Holly Hopkinson shouldn't be artistically swooshing around the streets of Notting Hill with Aleeshaa, drinking CAPPUCCINOS – like everyone else in the world.

It's *so* not fair. I really *need* that smartphone now because Aleeshaa is useless at replying to letters.

The second thing that is making me miserable is **Team Mean** AKA my brother and sister.

Harmony has stuck up this horrible sign on her bedroom door –

and is now vamoosing on a regular basis off to London with Mum. But will Mum let me go with them? NO.

Harold is no better. He gets to do nothing when Dad is doing nothing, and then he goes off with Dad – leaving me on my own to mind none of any business that I don't have.

And then to add flipping insult to the stale icing on the cake, **Team Mean** take the mickey out of *me* for hanging out with Vinnie.

But I have been abandoned in a land of sheep poo without a phone, so what am I supposed to do?

Befriend the CHICKENS?

Vinnie is basically my only option, friend-wise.

OK, so on the one hand Vinnie doesn't say a lot of words in the right order – but I think we're beginning to communicate via osmosis. And he *can talk* very well with animals. He's a modern-day Doctor Dolittle.*

Animals really like Vinnie.

So when the animals have a revolution like in Mum's book-club book, and decide to do in all the humans, I think Vinnie will be spared – and I'm going to stick with him as a long-term *Vin*surance policy.

Vinnie told me about Grandpa's pony, Beanstalk.

Dear, oh dear, oh dear.

Grandpa thought she was a baby carthorse when he bought her. But it turns out she's a flipping miniature Shetland pony, and according to Vinnie her legs are small – even for one of those. She couldn't pull a supermarket shopping trolley, let alone the cart in the farmyard.

* DOCTOR DOLITTLE – someone in history who did practically nothing except talk to animals.

Vinnie said he'll teach me to ride something a bit bigger one day if I like, but I said,

'NO WAY, JOSÉ.'

Vinnie can also drive a tractor, so if I need anything moving, he'll be the first to know.

FARMYARD NEWS – I think that Grandpa's plan for his foal, High Five, is a clear sign that Grandpa is not all there in the head department. As if proof was needed of *that* after the doofus decision to buy Beanstalk in the first place.

Grandpa saw me and Vinnie looking at High Five, so he wandered over to chew the cud, like farmers do.

'He's a beauty, Holly, isn't he? His dad is a stallion called Royal Approval, and this little fella will make us our FORTUNE.'

'Are you sure about that, Grandpa?' I asked.

'Oh yes,' he replied, spitting the piece of straw he was eating out on to the grass. 'OH YES.'

And then High Five sprinted round the paddock like a lunatic, bucking and kicking and going spit-spot faster than Beanstalk.

'See how quick he is?' Grandpa asked. 'He's leaving Beanstalk in the dust.'

'Well, sort of,' I agreed. 'But then Beanstalk is a miniature Shetland pony with unusually short legs . . . so I don't think we should get the TV crews in just yet.'

When we were in one of the top fields near the village, I asked Vinnie, 'You go to the school that I'm going to next term, don't you?'

And he replied, 'SOMETIMES.'

What sort of an answer is *that*?

CHAPTER 8

DIG IN HOLLY TIME

~~~~~

GRANDPA IS TEACHING ME ABOUT
HORSE RACING, WHICH IS UNEXPECTEDLY
HIS *BIG* THING –
VERY BIG THING, IN FACT.

He's even started calling me his Racing
Associate, a job title that I think should
definitely come with a free phone. (I will have
to press Grandpa on this.)

HOLLY HOPKINSON
(RACING ASSOCIATE)

Anyway, I heard Mum say to Dad that she thinks
Grandpa is a 'bad influence' – but any influence is a
bonus in the world of Holly Hopkinson right now.

Perhaps Mum and Dad might like to think about influencing me a bit too – isn't that what parents are *supposed* to do to their youngest child, *thank you very much*?

SOCIAL NEWS – I don't know why Grandpa puts up with Vera, who comes round as many days as she pleases. She's quite annoying, and a bit of a busybody. Always muttering and tut-tutting when we're studying the *Racing Post*. And she pulls faces when Beanstalk comes into the kitchen looking for treats.

(SOMETIMES BEANSTALK LEAVES HER A LITTLE PRESENT ON THE FLOOR.)

But Grandpa is a very patient man.

When I say Grandpa is teaching me about horse racing, I don't mean he actually races horses. No. He watches them on the TV and studies the *Racing Post*, and bets on which one will win. Grandpa's system for picking the horses is quite complicated, so when I'm not sure I go for any jockeys wearing pink. I don't mean to BLOW MY OWN TRUMPET, but I think I get it right more often than he does.

PROBLEM NEWS – I'm going to ask Grandpa for a lot more transparent-cy* if we're going to be racing associates. At the moment, we pick the horses together in the morning, *but* by the time he comes back from the village to 'see a man about a dog' and rings his mate Paddy Power after lunch, our selections have often been changed around.

If Grandpa is going to be incontinent,** he is **not** the sort of business partner I'm looking for, thank you very much.

PS Dad chopped some logs up today and came back in looking like someone had chucked a steaming **HOT** bucket of water over him.

'**WHO** DOESN'T NEED TO GO TO THE GYM TODAY?'

he asked.

* TRANSPARENT-CY – cutting out the jiggery-pokery (I heard Mum say this when she was showing off to someone on the phone the other day).

** INCONTINENT – lacking in self-control of your horse selections.

55

Quite clearly, *he* does. He's been outside for less than five minutes. I don't know if Lower Goring has sports facilities, but I suspect not.

THINGS LOWER GORING DOESN'T HAVE

- ✖ Restaurants
- ✖ Cafés
- ✖ Mobile-phone shops
- ✖ Corner shops
- ✖ Parks
- ✖ Social-service offices

CHAPTER 9

DAY BEFORE MY OFFICIAL BIRTHDAY

DAD HAS STARTED BRIBING HAROLD WITH BISCUITS TO COME OUT OF HIS BEDROOM AND CHOP THE LOGS WHILE DAD (AKA MR SOFA LOAFER) DRINKS CUPS OF TEA AND WATCHES COOKERY PROGRAMMES ON TV.

Unsurprisingly, Harold has made a BAD DEAL with Dad.

So, in my new and highly professional business-partner manner, I said, 'Excuse you . . . I'll be your agent and negotiate a better deal if you give me half of the upside.' (The difference between what he's getting now and what I think I can get him, *obviously.*) But Harold just put his headphones back on, grunted a bit more than usual and bunked off back to his bedroom.

He must have said something to Harmony, though, because she started doing a protest to Dad, saying it's child labour, which is illegal under the Geneva Contention.* She's threatening to report him to the authorities (Mum), even though Harold is quite obviously old enough to hit things with an AXE if he feels like it.

DEMONSTRATION NEWS –

Harmony has abruptly shut down her demonstration, which makes me wonder if Dad's paid her off too.

Tomorrow is the Glorious Twelfth, according to Grandpa, which is the day when the GROUSE-shooting season starts, though it doesn't sound very glorious if you're a grouse.

However, and more importantly, tomorrow is also *my birthday* – I will be ten years old. But I'm not holding out any great hope on the present/party front.

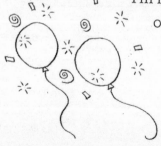

* GENEVA CONTENTION – when a bunch of people got together in Switzerland and had lunch.

Aunt Electra hasn't replied to my letter. But that isn't exactly the *ten o'clock news*. Dad says Aunt Electra is a bit bohemian.

Then Mum chucked in a 'really . . . and does everyone from Bohemia always forget to turn up on the right day when they're invited to anything?' in her 'SHARP' voice.

I don't think Mum and Aunt Electra are besties. But Dad and Aunt Electra get on like a house of fryer.**

There's no sign of Aleeshaa coming, either. And whenever I get time on Dad's laptop, she's never online. When I suggested to Mum that she might like to send up some smoke signals or something, as well as texting Aleeshaa's mum, she just said,

'IT'S TOO FAR FOR HER TO COME, HOLLY.'

Aleeshaa may well soon forget that I ever existed. But Mum has said there *is* going to be a bit of a surprise on my birthday.

** HOUSE OF FRYER – fish-and-chip shop.

POSSIBLE SURPRISES

☆ A brand-new smartphone
(OK, not a huge surprise
as it's top of my list)

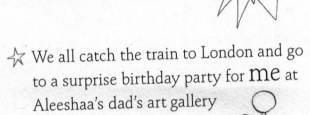

☆ We all catch the train to London and go
to a surprise birthday party for me at
Aleeshaa's dad's art gallery

THE BIRTHDAY EXPRESS

☆ Grandpa takes us to the races

SURPRISES THAT I
DO NOT WANT

☆ A children's entertainer who tells terrible jokes

☆ Dad dresses up as a clown (I have barely recovered from last time)

☆ Mum invites a bunch of kids who I don't know from the village school

☆ We go for a trip to somewhere in the countryside – we live there now, so there is no point in doing that.

HARMONY'S BIRTHDAY TREAT TO SEE THE LIONS AT LONGLEAT WAS THE WORST EVER. HAROLD WAS SICK ALL OVER US IN THE BACK OF THE CAR. IT WAS LIKE AN EXPLODING FIRE HOSE GOING OFF AND WE COULDN'T WIND THE WINDOWS DOWN IN CASE THE LIONS GOT IN.

I asked Harold and Harmony if they knew what my birthday surprise was going to be and whether there was anyone else we should invite. This was a MISTAKE

I WILL NOT BE MAKING AGAIN –

for reasons that will soon become

obvious . . .

CHAPTER 10

LIKE A WHITE SHEET FLOATING IN THE AIR

~~~~~~~~~~

IT'S MUCH EASIER TO GET TO SLEEP IN LONDON THAN THE COUNTRYSIDE.

There used to be a lovely, soothing TRAFFIC lullaby noise in our cul-de-sac, which made me nod off quicker than you can say 'Harry Potter'.

But around Lower Goring there's either deathly **silence**, wind singing creepy songs in the leaves of the trees or some animal shouting its head off as it tries to eat one of the villagers.

But as soon as I managed to stop thinking about the excitement of going back to Longleat (not) and the flipping owl outside my bedroom window had put a sock in it, I was off to the land of nod.

Then the next thing I heard was a knocking sound, which woke me up.

KNOCK. KNOCK . . . KNOCK. KNOCK.

To start with I thought it was the owl trying to get in. Then it started again.

And I knew it wasn't the owl.

The hairs stood up on the back of my neck.

'Is that you, Holly?' a spooky voice whispered. 'I am Mabel . . . Why haven't you invited me to your birthday party . . . I am *very* cross.'

Then I saw her appear in the doorway.

And then she started WHOOING .

I thought my heart was going to double-whopper explode – it was beating like Big Ben.

'YOU CAN COME IF YOU LIKE.'

I whispered, barely able to get the words out.

Grandpa hadn't been flipping joking about Mabel, after all. She was real, all right. About the same height as Harold.

'I am very cross with you, Holly,' Mabel repeated.

My mouth was so dry I couldn't speak, and I was shaking like a leaf.

Then I heard *Harold* laughing his head off. He was under a flipping white sheet, and Harmony was behind him doing the voice and the WHOOING.

'Thanks for the invite, little sis,' he cackled.

'BIRTHDAY SURPRISE!' Harmony laughed at me.

I am furious – absolutely furious. And I can't get back to sleep because I'm now certain that if Mabel does exist she is going to be absolutely flipping mad with the Hopkinson family for impersonating her. So it's just me, a potentially furious ghost upstairs, my memoir and that blooming owl hooting again outside.

WORST day-before-my-birthday EVER.

CHAPTER 11

MUM'S REJECT-PRESENT DRAWER

HOLLY HOPKINSON IS OFFICIALLY
TEN YEARS OLD. I AM NOW
PRACTICALLY A **TEENAGER**.

It happened to William Shakespeare and Milton (not sure if he had a surname), and now Holly Hopkinson. So now I'm nearly a teenager I feel my writing is a little **sharper**.

Mum's surprise didn't last very long – roughly about fifteen seconds after Harold and Harmony woke me up and made me look out of the window.

'IT'S, LIKE, KINDA **COOOOOL**,' Harmony purred like a cat.

'Yeah,' chimed in Harold, in an unexpectedly friendly voice. 'It's ROCK and ROLL, baby.'

'I am **not** a baby,' I reminded Harold.

Lots of Grandpa's canvas sheets had been tied up in the trees to make a sort of tent. And rugs and cushions laid out on the grass.

Not exactly a 'we're off to the Ritz to eat pancakes while you look at your new phone' sort of surprise. But Mum, Dad and Grandpa must have been working on it all night. And never mind, I thought. A smartphone might come along later in the day, if the delivery driver from the Amazon doesn't get lost and have to drive twice round the planet.

'We're having a special birthday lunch for you, Holly,' Mum announced when I got down for breakfast.

'Thank you, Mum,' I replied. 'Who's actually coming?'

'Well, Vinnie's going to come. And Dad's asked Vinnie's uncle, Vince.'

'We've all asked his uncle Vince,' Dad said quickly in his 'it wasn't me' voice.

Oh no. Vinnie's uncle could be a children's entertainer on the quiet when he isn't ploughing up turnips on the other side of the village and eating anything that can't run faster than him.

'Anyone from London? Aleeshaa?' I asked.

'Well, Aunt Electra's coming,' said Dad.

'If you're lucky,' said Mum under her breath, but I heard her. Still, that is

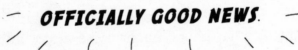

OFFICIALLY GOOD NEWS.

'And Vera's coming,' said Grandpa from behind the paper.

'And Mrs Smartside from the village says she might look in after she's seen to some fete business,' added Mum.

Whoopee –

thank God it's Vera and
this Mrs Smartside and
not Adele and Beyoncé –
do my parents know that
I'm ten years old today, I
wonder?

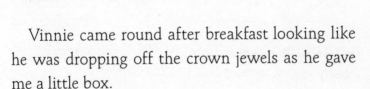

Vinnie came round after breakfast looking like
he was dropping off the crown jewels as he gave
me a little box.

'All riight. 'Tis for you, 'Olly,' he spluttered.

I opened it, and guess what was inside?

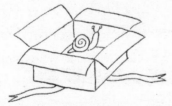

A snail.

Oh, man!

'If tho put it on thor tummy it'll come out of
shell after it gets used to tho and slither around.'

'Thank you, Vinnie,' I said, trying to use my
'appreciative' voice. 'It's just what I wanted. Where
will it live?'

'WITH THO.'

69

Then Dad gave me his present, which was wrapped up in Christmas paper because we've started recycling stuff as we're economising.*

RECYCLING works slightly differently on Grandpa's farm compared to city places. Mum is making a big fuss about putting plastic, paper and tins in bins, and the waste food into two different bins. The pigs are meant to have the waste food but not meat – obviously they shouldn't eat other animals, or themselves. But when Mum has gone to London, Grandpa just gives all the food to the pigs and takes the paper, tins and plastic up to his burning pit and chucks them all in together. Grandpa says I mustn't tell Mum – so something to store in the bribery locker there, **ah ha!**

'It's something for you when you get a bit older,' Dad said.

* ECONOMISING – not spending money on your children.

Since when do you give ten-year-olds a cookery book for their birthday present – and a *used* cookery book at that?

'IT'S A **HERITAGE** BOOK,'

he said, explaining the stains on the cover.

'Thank you, Dad,' I replied, trying to put on my 'happiest' face.

Dad gave me a lovely cuddle, which was actually the best present of the lot. But he has defo been having too much sofa-loafer time watching cookery programmes.

Halfway through the morning Vera turned up. She brought a big tin with her, which she rather obviously hid in the larder. I have a horrible feeling it might be a cake. Vera's food is INEDIBLE.

I've a good mind to ring up the bomb-disposal squad and tell them someone's left an unattended bag in our kitchen.

No sign of Aunt Electra yet, so I took Dad's cook book up to my room and read it for a while.

When I came back down, Mum said to Grandpa, 'Well, we're not going to let lunch get cold waiting for your daughter,' and Grandpa replied, 'I thought we were having salad.'

Actually, we had fish fingers for lunch, which are my favourite. I ate all the inside bits first and then saved the outside bits till last – taking the precaution to fake SNEEZE on them in case Harold thought he'd help himself. So things were looking up a bit.

Mum and Harmony gave me their presents after lunch. Harmony produced a Barbie doll.

CAME OUT OF MUM'S REJECT-PRESENT DRAWER

I GREW OUT OF BARBIE DOLLS YEARS AGO

Mum gave me rubber Wellington boots. She said, 'Now you're *such* good friends with Vinnie they will come in useful on the farm.'

Two things on that:

☆   I'm not that good friends with Vinnie. He is just a handy **temporary** friend and tactical ally for the start of school.

☆   The wellies are two sizes too big – Mum said, 'Never mind, you'll grow into them before you know it.' So will every spider this side of Chipping Topley.

THIS MAY WELL BE
THE OFFICIAL START OF
MY DARK YEARS.

CHAPTER 12

CHOCOLATE AND REINFORCED CONCRETE

I LET VINNIE BE MY MAIN OFFICIAL GUEST
OF HONOUR AT MY BIRTHDAY TEA IN THE
ABSENCE OF ALEESHAA AND AUNT ELECTRA.
DAD DID THE ENTERTAINMENT AND HE WAS
IN A FUNNY DOOFUS MOOD.

He showed Vince his trick of pulling the tablecloth off the table with all the glasses still on it, and this time it worked. But Mum failed miserably to eat ten dry crackers in five minutes.

Then Vinnie and I hid behind the 'tent' and started a new, secret language.
Given that Vinnie hasn't really mastered the words of his first language, I kept it pretty simple.

Here is some of our new code language – and Harmony and Harold, if you ever read my memoirs before they are *officially* published and see our secret words, I will do something really **BAD** to you.

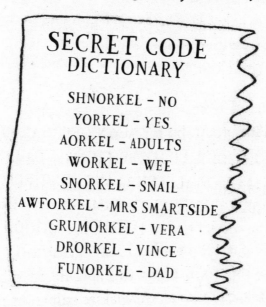

SECRET CODE
DICTIONARY

SHNORKEL – NO
YORKEL – YES
AORKEL – ADULTS
WORKEL – WEE
SNORKEL – SNAIL
AWFORKEL – MRS SMARTSIDE
GRUMORKEL – VERA
DRORKEL – VINCE
FUNORKEL – DAD

We might have to rethink this a bit, because we're getting muddled up between 'snail' and 'no'.

I wonder how long it took the Romans to make up their secret language? Mind you, they spent most of the day fooling around in massive baths, so they probably didn't have much time after that to do words before they went to bed.

Dad would have been a good Roman.

Then Mrs Smartside from the village arrived with a bunch of yapping dogs. Barkley did *not* like that and retreated to the kitchen, while Beanstalk bolted out of the kitchen back into her paddock. Moggy just stayed up a tree; Mum said she looked at all of us with disdain – whatever that is – probably something that Mum will be scrubbing tomorrow.

I heard Mum telling Dad, Grandpa and Vince to 'Calm it down.'

'Oh, how charming,' Mrs Smartside said as Mum rushed out with an armchair from the house to put in the 'tent'.

'We decided on a **Bedouin Arabian Nights** theme this year,' Mum said to Mrs Smartside, in her 'CREATIVE' voice. Which is palpable* rubbish because we've never had a theme before *ever* for *anything*.

And where in heaven's name are all the knights galloping around like lunatics and knocking each other's heads off with poles?

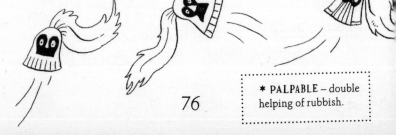

76

* **PALPABLE** – double helping of rubbish.

'Oh, Sally, you're so imaginative,' Mrs Smartside cooed.

'Well, you know,' said Mum. 'One has to be rather innovative in town.'

You'd think Mum had turned into J. K. Rowling, listening to the carry-on with Mrs Smartside.

Dad and Vince started sniggering like boys behind the bike shed.

'Oh, Holly,' Mrs Smartside said, 'I've bought you a little token.' And she *wasn't* kidding about the 'little'.

The Sellotape was more exciting than the token – and if she thinks I'm going to walk around wearing a badge that says 'MOTHER'S LITTLE HELPER' she can take a running jump with her flipping dogs all the way back to Lower Goring.

Then surprise visitors arrived from Chipping Topley – Mrs Chichester and her daughter, Daffodil. Mrs Chichester is on the fete committee and Daffodil goes to my new school! Here we go, I thought – the whole class will be invading in a minute and my village school career will be in ruins before it's even started.

When Mrs Chichester kisses people she just rubs her cheek (which smells of disgusting powder) next to theirs and goes, 'M-WAAAH.'

'How do you do?' I asked Daffodil.

'Fine, thank you,' she replied.

Then Daffodil handed me her present and said, 'It's a candle – you can never go wrong with a candle.'

TWO THINGS ON THAT:

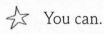 You can.

 The explosive excitement of unwrapping a candle is probably enhanced if you *don't* tell the person you're giving it to that it's a candle **before** they unwrap it.

'Nice clothes,' I said in my 'best manners' voice.

'Mum says they look good on me,' she replied in her 'Chipping Topley' voice.

MRS CHICHESTER

DAFFODIL

SAME CLOTHES

Then Vinnie interrupted us to officially reveal that he has a secret den on the farm that he'll show me and Daffodil some time if we join his secret club. But he wouldn't tell us the password, so I'm not sure how this is going to work out.

Mum and Mrs Chichester talked about who could open the fete. (Mrs Smartside didn't say much – I'll bet she wouldn't be shy with a pair of scissors, though.)

Then Vera brought *my* birthday cake into the tent.

Dad shouted, 'Here comes Barnes Wallis,'* and Vera gave him a dirty look.

'What flavour ist?' asked Vinnie (long sentence for Vinnie).

'CHOCOLATE AND REINFORCED CONCRETE,' Dad shouted.

'Make a wish, Holly,' commanded Mum as I tried to cut the cake.

(NOTE TO SELF – GO TO CHINESE MARTIAL-ARTS CLASSES BEFORE CUTTING ANOTHER ONE OF VERA'S CAKES.)

'Only one?' I asked, puffing my head off. But I managed to get four in because the knife got stuck and it took Dad all his strength to pull it out.

* BARNES WALLIS – hero in film who dropped cakes and bombs on things.

MY WISHES WERE:

★ Dad gets a surprise new job in London – full time.

 ★ A cake from the corner shop near where we lived in London.

★ Aunt Electra or Aleeshaa to arrive.

Sorry it's late!

★ The driver from the Amazon to turn up with my flipping smartphone.

Then Harold appeared in his own sweet time from his bedroom.

'Happy birthday, little sis,' he said in his 'stupid' voice that he thinks sounds like a ROCK STAR. 'I've been on it today . . . but here's the good news.'

'YOU'RE LEAVING HOME?' I said.

'Hey . . . I've written this great song and I'm going to give **you** half the royalties as your birthday present . . . What do you say to that?'

'Excuse you . . . where's the paperwork?' is what I said to that.

He's such a doofus.

I WISH AUNT ELECTRA
WAS HERE.

CHAPTER 13

A CLASH OF VULTURES

WELL, PART OF MY **THIRD WISH** ONLY TOOK ABOUT HALF AN HOUR TO COME TRUE, WHICH BODES WELL FOR THE FUTURE. THE **MIST OF GLOOM** IS LIFTING.

Aunt Electra came belting down the lane in her red open-top sports car. Which looks very cool until you see it up close and notice all the rust patches and the wooden wheels.

'Darling Holly . . . Happy, happy birthday . . . and such a special one too,' Aunt Electra said as I hugged her. She smelled lovely. Like a big marshmallow. With just a slight whiff of EXHAUST. Finally, someone seemed to be excited about *my* birthday.

'So who have we here?' asked Aunt Electra, looking around Mum's Arabian Nights Bedouin tent.

'HELLO, ELECTRA,' Mum said.

'Darling Sally . . . sorry I'm a tad late . . . traffic was absolutely horrendous. Hello, I'm Electra,' she said, wafting at Mrs Smartside, which made Mrs Smartside's nose recoil.

'Are you, indeed?' replied Mrs Smartside. 'I don't believe we've had the pleasure.' Mrs Smartside was as frosty as an iceberg on International Iceberg Day. She certainly was not feeling any pleasure.

'Cup of tea to refresh you, Electra?' asked Dad.

'No, thank you, darling . . . but a pink martini wouldn't go amiss . . . I've left the ingredients in the kitchen, if you'd be a dear and make one for me.'

Mum's eyebrows looked as if they were trying to go into hiding behind her ears.

Aunt Electra got her noggin into her glass and demolished a couple of pink martinis. Then she said, in a promisingly 'secretive' voice,

'HOLLY . . . SHALL WE GO AND HAVE A WANDER AROUND THE GARDEN?'

Aunt Electra has never been interested in gardening, as far as I know, so I was hoping this might be a birthday present situation.

She was carrying her big bag that she keeps everything in; she even had her own teapot in there once.

'How are you, Holly?' she asked when we were alone.

'Fine,' I lied. One thing I do know is that when adults ask you how you are, they don't actually want to know.

'HOW'S LIFE ON THE FARM? IS ANYONE LOOKING AFTER YOU?'

I was beginning to wonder if this was some sort of quiz game.

So I told a porky and said that life on the farm was fine, because I hadn't worked out the rules of her game. You've got to be one step ahead when you're playing games with adults.

Then she asked me if I'd made any friends, and I said, 'Well, Vinnie comes round most days, but he's only temporary until I make some proper friends.' Then I added, 'Look, Aunt Electra, you're going to have to tell me the rules, cos I haven't the foggiest as to what's going on with all these questions.'

So she said, 'Holly, your letter worried me *terribly*; but I've got something for you which will help you cope.'

And then I felt guilty, as all that my letter was meant to do was:

☆ Get her to come to my party.
☆ Get her to bring a phone with her.

Anyway, she then **cut to the chase**, as they say in Bolivia.

'Holly . . . I'm going to give you a very special birthday present . . . one that will help you navigate* the troubled waters of life.'

And I thought,

DOUBLE-WHOPPER
BINGO TOPLEY,
THIS SOUNDS LIKE IT'S GOING TO BE
A SMARTPHONE.

SPOILER ALERT: it wasn't a smartphone.
It was something *much* more
EXCITING than that.

* **NAVIGATE** – don't know what she's on about – probably to do with Grandpa's gates.

CHAPTER 14

WATCH OUT, WORLD

AUNT ELECTRA GLANCED AROUND THE
GARDEN LIKE A JEWEL THIEF, AND THEN
SHE PULLED AN OLD LEATHER BELT
OUT OF HER BAG.

'Oh . . . thank you, Aunt Electra . . . it's just
what I wanted,' I said in my 'disappointed best
manners' voice.

'HAVE A LOOK INSIDE
ITS SECRET POUCH,
YOU GOOSE,' she instructed.

And, sure enough, there was a secret pocket
inside the belt with something quite solid inside.
I had a quick scrabble about and out came a gold
chain; and on the end of it was a gold pocket
watch. The sort that *old* people wear, thank you
very much. Make that *very old*.

AS IF I CARE WHAT
THE TIME IS. AND I DON'T
WANT TO BANG ON ABOUT
SMARTPHONES,
BUT THEY DO
THE TIME TOO.

I tried to put my happiest face on, but acting isn't my strongest thing.

'Holly,' Aunt Electra said. 'I know Harmony gets to spend more time with Mum than you do; and Dad and Harold hang out too, so this Magic Pocket Watch will be your guardian . . . your helper.'

'DID YOU SAY "MAGIC"?' I asked.

'I did, Holly,' Aunt Electra said. 'If you wave it in front of anyone's nose, you can HYPNOTISE them . . . and make them do things! But it has slightly got a mind of its own . . . If it doesn't think it's being used as a force for *good* or *fun* it won't play ball.'

I thought she'd gone mad – or drunk too many martinis.

'What do you mean "play ball", Aunt Electra?'

'Well . . . the magic won't work if the Pocket Watch doesn't think you're asking for something that's either good or fun.'

'Are you actually messing with me, Aunt Electra?' I asked in my 'I'm not a doofus' voice.

She shook her head like a witch's cat.

 'THIS WATCH . . . CAN MAKE PEOPLE DO WHAT I WANT?'

'YES.'

It began to dawn on me that Aunt Electra had come up with a double-whopper top present.

'Crikey . . . How long can I keep it for?'

'As long as you want it.'

'Really . . . ? How long have you had it for?'

'Since my mother – your grandma – gave it to me.'

'Grandma Esme?' I'd never met her, so she must have died when I was very little. When I asked Dad about her, he said, 'Best let sleeping dogs lie,' which was strange, because if my grandma was a dog then the family is even WEIRDER than I thought. Though it would explain some of the smells Harold makes.

'Yes,' said Electra.

'Why don't you use it to make Mum nicer to you?'

Aunt Electra smiled. 'It doesn't quite work like that.'

'And Grandma Esme. What did she use it for?'

'Well, she was often trying to get Grandpa to do things he didn't always feel like doing . . . but most of the time the MAGIC POCKET WATCH agreed with Grandpa. So it didn't work. When we left New York in a bit of a hurry—'

'Whoa . . . back up there, Aunt Electra,' I said in my 'traffic cop' voice. *'New York?'*

'Yes . . . New York . . . don't you know about Grandpa, Grandma, me and your dad being there?'

(You could have knocked me over with the Statue of Liberty.)

'Dad has never mentioned New York.'

'Well, we were very young, and when we left, Grandma Esme didn't come with us—'

'Stop . . . stop . . . stop . . . I didn't know that either.'

'Well, where did you think she was?'

'Heaven.'

Aunt Electra gave a crazy bohemian laugh.

'Try Vegas more like . . . anyway . . . where was I?'

'Esme . . . Grandpa . . . the MAGIC POCKET WATCH!' I said, smelling that something FISHY has been going on and no one has told me about it.

'Oh yes . . . Well, obviously I was very young when Grandma Esme handed me the **MAGIC POCKET WATCH** on the quay. She said she hoped it would look after me.'

Aunt Electra was beginning to look a bit weepy, which was embarrassing, so I let 'New York' go for the time being.

What have *you* used it for, Aunt Electra?'

'Well, let's just say I had some friends who needed a bit of hypnotising . . . and I used it to help them.'

'In Bohemia?'

'No, Hampshire, actually.'

'How does it work?'

Aunt Electra looked a bit tired.

'I'll show you tomorrow,' she said. 'Right now it's time for another pink martini.'

'Thank you, Aunt Electra, it will never leave me,' I promised in my 'very pleased' voice.

'Holly, it's yours as long as you want it to be . . . but remember it must only be used for *good* or *fun* . . . maybe that was where Grandma Esme went wrong . . . and you *must* pass it on to a female member of our family. As I have to you, my darling girl.'

I nodded like Barkley does when the meat adverts are on the telly. But my mind was already BUZZING like a bewitched bee.

When we got back to the tent, Mrs Smartside had gone and *my* birthday party was in

full swing.

It had been a long day for my parents, but it had all ended very well.

WATCH OUT, WORLD –
HERE COMES
MAGIC
HOLLY HOPKINSON.

CHAPTER 15

IMPLEMENTATION

BY THE TIME AUNT ELECTRA HAULED
HERSELF OUT OF BED THE NEXT MORNING,
MUM WAS LONG GONE FOR LONDON,
DAD WAS IMMERSED IN SOME COOKERY
PROGRAMME AND GRANDPA, AS USUAL, WAS
BURIED IN THE *RACING POST.*

I was *bursting* at the seams to get hypnotising stuff. My life was about to change forever. I had been daydreaming about a few things that I could do with my new POWERS. Such as:

☆ Get me a smartphone THIS INSTANT !!

☆ Get all the kids at school to like me instantly and want to be my friend (well, the cool ones, obviously)

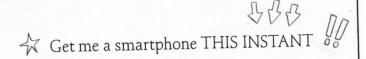

☆ Convince Aleeshaa to move to the countryside

☆ Get someone to build hotels for farm animals with full facilities so they don't have to do their business all over the floor

☆ Get Mabel to haunt Harold for the rest of his life

☆ Get someone to give Dad a London job

☆ Get Harmony to protest about something that's actually worth protesting about

For her breakfast Aunt Electra mixed a raw egg with lashings of Worcestershire sauce and, after gargling like a charging bull and shouting, 'Down the hatch,' she swallowed it in one go. Any raw eggs in the vicinity of Aunt Electra have a short life expectancy.

'Right, Holly,' she said. 'While the coast is clear we'd better get down to work . . . let's test it out on an animal . . . Any suggestions?'

'Well, I suppose there's always Barkley,' I said.

He was sitting on the sofa as enthralled as Dad in some recipe. He must be the only dog in the world that can smell food on the television.

'Good,' agreed Aunt Electra. 'So what would be very difficult to get Barkley to do?'

'Well, he doesn't do anything, really, except eat . . . That's all he's interested in . . . that and the poodle he used to chat up in the park in London.'

'Excellent . . . Well, let's take Barkley and a plate of his favourite food down to the bottom of the garden, shall we?'

'That's steak,' I informed Aunt Electra. 'Which Grandpa is meant to be having for his lunch.'

'Perfect,' she said.

*This is going to be a fiasco,** I thought as I hid the steak in Aunt Electra's bag.

So the three of us went to the bottom of the garden, looking as if we were about to rob a bank.

I slipped my right hand into my new belt and fished out my MAGIC POCKET WATCH. In the cold light of day I was feeling pretty silly about all this, but Aunt Electra wasn't *acting* like it was all a terrible prank at my expense, so I was going along with it.

Aunt Electra told me to make Barkley sit.

* FIASCO – Mum always says Harold's room is a fiasco, so something minging that stinks.

'Right . . . this is the important bit, Holly . . . you've got to wave the **MAGIC POCKET WATCH** backwards and forwards, forwards and backwards in front of his nose . . . and slowly say,

"SPIRO, SPERO, SQUIGGLEOUS SCOTCH,

CAST YOUR EYES WHITHER MY WATCH.'"

'Right . . .' I said, in my 'pull-the-other-one' voice.

'Seriously,' said Aunt Electra. 'The watch was made in the eighteenth century by a Scottish watchmaker and amateur **SORCERER**. He was . . . a little **ECCENTRIC**.'

'OK . . .' I said. Anyone *she* was calling eccentric must have been flat-out weird.

Electra watched me with her beady eyes. 'If you say it too fast or too slow, things can go wrong . . . and, depending on how susceptible the person is, you have to say it the right number of times.'

'What exactly do you mean, "go wrong"?'

Aunt Electra pulled a face like she was swallowing another raw egg with Worcestershire sauce.

'Well, let's just give it a try and see what happens, shall we?'

So I started on Barkley, nice and slowly, and repeated the funny rhyme three times.

'SPIRO, SPERO, SQUIGGLEOUS SCOTCH, CAST YOUR EYES WHITHER MY WATCH.'

I had not expected the **MAGIC POCKET WATCH** to be so heavy – it weighs a lot more than you'd think.

'Very good,' said Aunt Electra. 'That was nice and slow . . . and three is about right.'

'About?'

It all sounded very hit-and-miss to me. This could go double-whopper spanner in the works if I guess wrong.

Anyway, Barkley kept his eyes on the watch as if it was a pot of swinging giblets.

'Right,' Aunt Electra said, 'now put that juicy steak on the grass in front of him, and tell him *not* to eat it.'

'Is this going to be my fault if Barkley eats Grandpa's lunch?' I asked.

'Have faith, Holly,' she replied.

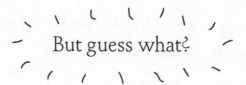

Once Barkley looked GOGGLE-EYED, I told him not to eat the steak, and put it on the ground – waiting for Barkley to make his lunch-ending lurch.

But guess what?

He just sat there, nodding like Harold does when he's got his speakers on. And he *just looked* at it.

'OH, MY GOODNESS . . .
THAT IS MAGIC,'   I said.

'Yes,' said Aunt Electra in her 'unstably excited' voice. 'It is.'

Oh, boy, this is going to be SEISMIC!

Life changing, in fact.

'Good start,' said Aunt Electra. '*Now* you need to have a go on a human.'

GULP.

CHAPTER 16

OVERCOOKED

'REALLY . . .' I SAID HESITANTLY.
'A HUMAN?'

'HAVE CONFIDENCE, HOLLY . . .
A HUMAN WILL BE FINE.'

But as luck would have it, a halfway house option came poking his nose round the corner – Vinnie.

'He'll do,' said Aunt Electra. 'What doesn't Vinnie like doing?'

'Talking, I suppose,' I suggested.

'Perfect,' she said, fishing a book out of her bag. 'Let's get him to read some Shakespeare.'

'Are you kidding?' I laughed.

104

'We shall see,' said Aunt Electra with a flourish of her hand. 'Vinnie, come here, darling,' she shouted, and he sloped over.

'Er, Vinnie,' I said, waving my **MAGIC POCKET WATCH** in front of his nose, 'look at my new watch.'

'ALL RIIGHT,' he said.

And then, slightly nervously – even though it was only Vinnie – I tried out the weird mantra three times.

'SPIRO, SPERO, SQUIGGLEOUS SCOTCH, CAST YOUR EYES WHITHER MY WATCH.'

Vinnie blinked a bit as his eyes went backwards and forwards. Then Aunt Electra gave me the nod.

'Vinnie, you will read us Shakespeare, if you please,' I commanded in my 'Hamlet' voice, handing him Aunt Electra's book. Vinnie took the book, but I didn't think he'd be able to read it, let alone spout it out. But then off he went.

'To be or not to be: that is the question: whether 'tis nobler in the mind to suffer the slings and arrows of outrageous fortune, or to take arms against a sea of troubles.'

'CRIKEY,' I said.

'HE'S GONE BONKERS.'

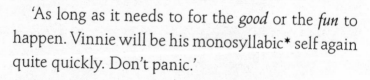

'Um . . .' said Aunt Electra. 'I think we may have overcooked Vinnie a bit.'

'*Overcooked him?* How long does the magic last for?'

'As long as it needs to for the *good* or the *fun* to happen. Vinnie will be his monosyllabic* self again quite quickly. Don't panic.'

'You OK?' I asked Vinnie a few minutes later, after he'd come back down from his orbiting.

* MONOSYLLABIC – a single person like Vinnie who says short words.

‘ALL RIIGHT,’ he replied.

Aunt Electra was right – he was back to his old self. But that was a bit alarming.

‘You run along then, Vinnie, there's a good boy,’ said Aunt Electra.

Vinnie peered at her. ‘All riiight,’ he said, and wandered off, oblivious to the scientific experiment that he'd just taken part in.

This was *amazing*.

I was now

HOLLY HOPKINSON
(HYPNOTIST)

The world was going to be my OCTOPUS, as they say in Dad's old films.

CHAPTER 17

NOT VERY SUSCEPTIBLE

'THAT WAS AMAZING!'
I SAID. 'WHAT SHALL WE TRY NEXT?'

'Well, Vera is bound to be in the kitchen baking a weapon of mass destruction . . . let's try her?' said Aunt Electra.

So off we went to locate Vera. My legs broke into a sort of skip that they do when they're feeling very happy. It's like a half walk, half CANTER. And my right index finger and thumb click in time with my left foot . . . until they got to the kitchen.

I swallowed. Vera was a bit daunting, even for a streetwise London kid like me. 'Can't we try one of the sheep?' I asked Aunt Electra. 'The worst it can do is spray everyone with black pellets from its bottom.'

'No, Holly . . . you're doing fine . . . you just need more practice.'

Aunt Electra watched through the window and I gave it a go.

'Vera, look what Aunt Electra has given me,' I said. And I wiggled my MAGIC WATCH backwards and forwards in front of Vera's nose and gave her three verses of 'SPIRO, SPERO'.

'What is the matter with you, child?' Vera snapped.

'Er . . . Vera, you will stop giving Grandpa earache about selling the cows, and go home,' I commanded with a bit of a flourish.

'I'll do no such thing,' she said, giving me a Nothern stare. 'NOW, CLEAR OFF.'

Aunt Electra was sitting in the Bedouin tent laughing her head off when I found her.

'Excuse you,' I said. 'Thank you *very* much indeed. That's a fine mess you got me into there.'

I do *not* mind admitting that it took Aunt Electra some time to calm me down . . .

It turns out that Vera is as tough as old boots, and probably needs at least five or six verses to get her under control. Apparently she is what adults call, 'not very susceptible'.

'Let's try again,' said Aunt Electra. 'We'll go for someone a bit easier this time. Where's your dad?'

Dad was watching TV, of course, with his mini-me Harold sitting beside him.

'OK,' said Aunt Electra. 'Give him three verses.'

So I waited for the woman who's eaten all her recipes to come on in the advert break; Harold went off somewhere else to SCRATCH, so I waved the MAGIC POCKET WATCH in front of Dad's nose three times.

'SPIRO, SPERO, SQUIGGLEOUS SCOTCH,
CAST YOUR EYES WHITHER MY WATCH.'

Dad does so much screen time he seemed perfectly happy to mindlessly gaze at my watch going backwards and forwards.

'On Monday you will take me rural freelancing with you,' I told Dad. 'Even it's a quiet day in that part of the global economy.'

(YOU SEE, I WANT TO FIND OUT WHAT HE'S GETTING UP TO ON HIS **MYSTERIOUS** TRIPS TO THE VILLAGE. AND IT'S ABOUT TIME HE MADE SOME EFFORT WITH ME TOO, THANK YOU VERY MUCH. I MAY BE THE YOUNGEST DAUGHTER, BUT I AM **FLESH AND BLOOD**.)

'Yes, Holly,' he replied. 'Of course . . . that would be a pleasure.'

Aunt Electra had a doubtful look on her face.

'Holly, is that either *fun* or a force for *good*?' she asked me in her 'HUSHED' voice afterwards.

'I'm not sure if it's going to be fun . . . but it will be for the good in the long run, I think . . .

for me, anyway!'

CHAPTER 18

THE CHEQUERS BUSINESS CENTRE

DAD HAS STOPPED GOING OUT RURAL FREELANCING IN THE MORNINGS FULL STOP. SO I'M STILL WAITING TO KNOW IF MY HYPNOSIS WORKED ON HIM, OR IF ELECTRA IS PLAYING SOME KIND OF ELABORATE PRANK ON ME TO MAKE ME LOOK LIKE A DOOFUS.

Vera is getting her knickers in a twist about Dad hanging about all morning watching cookery programmes and saying, 'I'll have a cuppa if you're making one, Vera.' Mainly, I think, because she likes watching the really trashy stuff on one of the other channels where everyone talks about how ROTTEN their families are. At this rate *we'll* be on one of those shows – I can just see it now . . .

PRESENTER (loving every minute of it):

'So, Holly . . . what has gone wrong with your family?'

ME: 'Well, my dad's addicted to cookery programmes, my mum got injured on a train fooling around, my brother's lost the power of communication and my sister has been kidnapped by someone she was protesting about. And then there's my grandpa, who should be old enough to know better . . . he broke our TV by throwing something at it the other day.'

HOLLY HOPKINSON
ONE GIRL'S STRUGGLE WITH TROUBLESOME FAMILY

I need to find out if you can get addicted to cookery programmes. It's not like Dad even cooks.

'Bye, Dad,' I shouted as I left the house. 'I'm just off to play with . . . erm . . . Vinnie.'

'Don't do anything I wouldn't do,' Dad shouted back cheerily. 'I'll see you later. I'm off in a minute to go to some meetings.'

'About time too,' grumbled Vera, who was Dyson-ing around Dad's feet just to annoy him.

But the **MAIN BUSINESS NEWS** today is: I decided to do some persuasion on Vinnie to get to the bottom of Grandpa's meetings with men about dogs.

I met him outside the barn where the tractor is kept.

'HELLO, VINNIE.'

'ALL RIIGHT,' he said.

'How close does Grandpa's farm get to the village?'

'Top field next to village,' Vinnie advised, very nearly completing an entire sentence.

'Well, I've changed my mind about you teaching me to drive the tractor,' I said. 'Let's drive it up to the field next to the village.'

Vinnie was delighted.

114

'Wait for me here,' I shouted to Vinnie as I leaped off the tractor and beetled towards the gate at the top of the field. Good job I did PE at my London school. That gate hasn't been opened for donkey's years, so I had to climb over it.

Halfway down the path to the village I came across a big pile of horse **POO**.

Steaming.

WHIFFING like anything.

Not a nice stink at all.

Definitely done that morning.

↑
DISGUSTING

Someone needs to do something about that. I could have stepped right in it. No bins or bags anywhere. I'll have to mention it to Harmony – she can protest about it.

Anyway, there's a big hedge in the middle of the village at the bottom of the garden of Lower Goring Hall. The hall is actually a massive house, not a hall; but double-whopper ruined by some doofus who let it fall down – no one has lived there for years.

So it's a handy hiding place if you're spying, as it's opposite a building called the Chequers – which looks a bit like a middle-sized country house with funny wobbly windows.

I didn't have to wait long until Grandpa arrived. But guess *who* was with him?

YES.

My dad – so **this** is where he goes to do his rural freelancing, I realised. The Chequers must be like a country business centre – I've seen one in London – you can rent a 'HOT DESK' by the week and use a meeting room where they do surfing lessons and internet talking and stuff like that.

I'll have to tell Harmony and Harold about this situation because they'll get much faster broadband in there. Better than standing on one leg in Harmony's bedroom.

There will be a fee for that information – I'm not giving my knowledge away for free, thank you very much.

But what I need to know is – what is Grandpa doing at Dad's freelancing place?

Holly Hopkinson is very CONFUSED – which is not good for my life expectancy – but I get the feeling that revelations are about to start

falling from
the sky.

CHAPTER 19

GRANDPA'S LITTLE EARNER

If these memoirs come to a sudden halt, it's because I'm in **PRISON**. I'd like to point out that it wasn't my idea. I just had to go along with it.

So about midday I was minding my own business and doing one of my so-called voluntary and thus unpaid holiday jobs – which was scooping up cow poo and making them into bricks to put on the fire when they dry out. Dad says it's only processed grass – but I don't see him up to his elbows in **POO**.

Mum had got the early train to London – it's all right for some – and took Harmony with her. My older sister is naturally going to go and demonstrate outside some embassy about something being unfair – poor them.

Harold was meant to be on brick duty with me, but he did a **MOODY** vanishing act – up to his bedroom knocking seven bells out of his drum kit.

↑

(I WOULD PUT A COMPLAINT IN TO THE LOCAL COUNCIL, BUT I *DO* HAVE FINANCIAL CONSIDERATIONS NOW HE'S WRITTEN A SONG FOR ME.)

Then Dad finally went out to do some rural freelancing. **Not** in a suit again, I noticed.

Grandpa – as usual – was looking at the *Racing Post*, before, I thought, heading off to the Chequers for his now un-secret secret rendezvous with Dad. But I was WRONG about that, as it turned out.

Vera was making black pudding, which is 100% DISGUSTING and is the most revolting pudding I've ever eaten, no matter how much cream and sugar you put on it.

Then it started to rain and Vinnie showed up.

'All riight,' Vinnie said.

'Yorkel . . . what are you up to, Vinnie?' I asked. 'Want to help me make POO bricks?'

'S'RAINING,' Vinnie said.

'Yes, Vinnie, I *can* see that.'

'S'raining . . . so got to help yer man.'

So I followed Vinnie into the kitchen.

'Ah, Holly . . . you going to come and help us?' Grandpa asked jovially, without a hint of CRIME in his voice.

'If you like, Grandpa,' I said foolishly. And this is what happened.

There's a road at the top of the farm that goes from Lower Goring to London via Chipping Topley – so it's a big deal. Lots of traffic comes past. And it goes through a big dip right beside Grandpa's fields. Which was probably a favourite spot for highwaymen* in the old days.

The verges on either side of the road are very steep. (I think Grandpa may have something to do with that.)

There are little channels either side of the road that are meant to let the water drain away when it rains – which Grandpa and Vinnie block up *on purpose*. And then they unblock another channel in the hedge which lets the water from one of Grandpa's fields flood the road ...

* HIGHWAYMEN – men from the council who steal stuff from people stuck in traffic jams.

'Right, you two hide in the hedge. I'll be in my normal spot, Vinnie,' Grandpa said before driving off on his tractor. By now I was pretty WET and not a happy bunny, I can tell you.

'*What* are we doing?' I asked Vinnie.

'Tho will see,' he said. His poor grasp of spoken English language was really getting on my nerves. I'm beginning to wonder if he's even temporary countryside best-friend material.

'Have you done this before, Vinnie?' I asked.

'Yorkel . . . every time it rains,' he replied, shrugging his shoulders.

A few minutes later a car came bombing along, slammed straight into the water and ground to a coughing halt. At which point Vinnie sprang out of the hedge and wandered along the road whistling like an escaped LUNATIC.

'All riight?' Vinnie asked the driver, who was anything but all right now that his car had conked out.

'Need tractor to get tho to village?' asked Vinnie. The driver nodded appreciatively.

'THAT'LL BE **TEN POUND**.'

What the driver didn't know was that ten pounds only got him an introduction to Grandpa, who *just* happened to be round the corner with his tractor. (Grandpa is a lousy actor, by the way.) Grandpa then fleeced the man for a lot more to actually tow him to the village.

'It's like a public service,' Grandpa told me. 'We stop people driving too fast – like speed bumps. And then we help them get to the village. Two good deeds wrapped into one. But there's no need to tell any of the others, though . . . *especially* your mother,' he said. 'The thing is, Holly . . . farming isn't what it once was and I've got to "keep the wolf from the door",' Grandpa added.

So I think the whole thing is about fencing for the chicken coop.

I nodded and promised I wouldn't whisper a word to Mum, and he smiled. I'm pleased too because I now have more leverage* over Grandpa when we come to negotiate our Racing Associates business partnership. (I will make the recycling scandal the ICING on the negotiation cake.)

But I have unfortunately joined the CRIMINAL classes – so it may not be long before I end up in that prison – unless my MAGIC POCKET WATCH can sort things out vis-à-vis the law.

PS I've been thinking about Grandpa. I know that he gets up to something in the Chequers Business Centre, quite possibly with Dad – and that he is a modern-day HIGHWAYMAN – but there is still something else lurking in his character like an unexploded World War Two bomb that I can't put my finger on. And what about this used-to-live-in-New York stuff that Aunt Electra let slip – excuse you? Hardly normal behaviour for a farmer from the Chipping Topley area.

* LEVERAGE – way of extracting maximum possible bribe.

He might look like a farmer, smell like a farmer and eat like a farmer – but I don't think he knows the first thing about actual farming.

FOR MIGRANT TEN-YEAR-OLDS –
EVEN IF THEY ARE

TRAINEE HYPNOTISTS.

CHAPTER 20
THE VILLAGE CULTURAL EVENTS ORGANISING COMMITTEE (VCEOC)

LOCAL NEWS –
MUM HAS DECIDED TO VOLUNTEER HER 'PR SKILLS' TO THE VILLAGE FETE.

The Village Cultural Events Organising Committee (VCEOC) are organising it. And guess who Mum's new best friend is?

YES.

Chairperson Mrs Smartside, of course.

Mrs Smartside lives in the big house next to the church, with a massive wall so you can't look in and see what's going on; or climb over it to get into her orchard, which they say has the best apples and plums in the Chipping Topley area.

She is very grand and always walks around the village telling everyone what to do while her terriers nip everyone's ankles, thank you very much.

If she tries to pull any stunts on me she might find that my MAGIC POCKET WATCH makes her put her underpants on over the top of her trousers.

Mrs Smartside is also the Chair of the Governors of the village school, so I need to watch it.

Mum sprang it on me that I've got the unfortunate job of handing out biscuits to everyone and sweeping up after her VCEOC meeting.

'I thought Harmony was your sidekick,' I said to Mum in my 'REBELLIOUS' voice.

'Don't be silly, Holly,' Mum replied in her 'really annoying adult' voice. What is silly about telling the truth?

NONCOMPREHENDO!

'So how much does it actually pay?' I asked.

'Nothing, Holly,' said Mum. 'It's volunteer work.'

Thank *you* very much. Since when did volunteering pay the bill for a smartphone?

I am FURIOUS.

Mum needs to take me more seriously if she wants future generations reading my memoirs to like her. It only takes the odd word from my pen to shape history.

But I have to admit I'm getting a pretty good opportunity to listen to the adults WAFFLING on, and it seems like they've totally forgotten I'm here in the kitchen once they get their hands on the Jaffa cakes.

'As you all know, the village school roof is leaking badly,' Mrs Smartside announced in her 'emergency' voice. 'And I'm afraid if it's not mended by the winter, Health and Safety have said we'll have to close the school.'

Gasps from everyone – and from me, though luckily the others gasping covered the sound of me gasping.

'Is there anything we can do?' Vera asked. 'Our Vinnie won't cope in a bigger school.'

You're not kidding! Vinnie can barely manage village speak – how on earth would he manage in a town school? And then I realised something else: this was **EMERGENCY NEWS** for me too – if Lower Goring's school closed down I would have to go to the big school with Harmony in Chipping Topley,

and that would be *a lot worse*!

'As a matter of fact there is something we can do,' said Mrs Smartside. 'We must raise as much as possible at this year's fete, and of course the school Christmas show as well.'

'Might need Miss Bossom to do something a bit more exciting, then,' someone muttered.

'It wasn't exactly a box-office smash last year, was it?' agreed another voice.

'It were boring,' echoed Vince.

'Now, now,' said Mrs Smartside. 'I'm sure Miss Bossom will do her best. Let's get down to fete business. ITEM ONE, the Tough Farmer Challenge: Vince, can you fill us in?'

It turns out that Vinnie's uncle Vince is the BIG CHEESE of the Tough Farmer competition.

'Same as last year,' said Vince. 'Bigley's are going to sponsor again . . . two classes . . . one for young farmers and their girlfriends, one for farmers and their wives.'

Then Mum cleared her throat. 'Oh . . . that's not very PC,' she said in a 'POSH' voice I've never heard her use before.

'YOU WHAT?' grunted Vince.

'Well, in this day and age, shouldn't it be "partners"?' Mum asked.

130

'Bigley's won't like it . . . they don't like that sort of thing,' Vince replied.

'That sort of thing? Excuse me, but I really must—'

'Well, let's not get bogged down. We've got a lot to get through,' snapped Mrs Smartside. 'ITEM NUMBER TWO . . . the cake stall. Vera, can you bring us up to speed?'

I had a peek through the kitchen hatch just as Mum jumped in again, with her new voice.

'Might I suggest, Angela (that's Mrs Smartside), that we could put a bit of a WOW factor into the cake stall this year and go live?'

'Go live?' said Vera, looking like she wanted to knock Mum's block off. 'GO LIVE?'

'How about a real-time cake bake-off. We could call it a "cake-off",' suggested Mum.

'OH, YOU'RE A GENIUS, SALLY,'

said Mrs Smartside. 'A breath of fresh air.'

The last thing Vera looked like she was breathing in at that point was fresh air, I can tell you. More like a bucket of something from the tank under the BOGS.

'Well, maybe we could have both,' said Mrs Smartside. 'Moving on. ITEM THREE . . . Mud-wrestling . . . Um, Vicar, I think this is your department.'

I couldn't believe my ears. The fat guy in a black T-shirt and jeans is *our* vicar. You've got to be joking.

'Yes, well, as you all know it got a bit out of hand last year, so we're not going to have the sixty-five and over class this time. But I'm pleased to report the chemist in Chipping Topley is very keen to be the sponsor again.'

'Not surprised,' chirped someone and everyone laughed. There's something going on there with the mud-wrestling –

NOTE TO SELF: Vinnie might know.

'Some decorum,* *please*,' Mrs Smartside said, clapping her hands. 'ITEM FOUR. Charmain . . . the floating ducks . . . how are we doing with them?'

Later, just as I thought we were in the clear, I got collared by Mum.

'Holly, Mrs Chichester is going to come over for tea one day . . . and she could bring Daffodil over too . . . won't that be nice.'

That was what Dad calls a rheumatoidical** question. ← (WHICH IS WHY I HAVEN'T PUT A QUESTION MARK AT THE END OF THAT SENTENCE.)

I sincerely hope there is more to Daffodil than her MATCHY MATCHY mum outfits. And that she realises I make for an excellent new friend, even though I have no smartphone to speak of. Hmmm, maybe she has one we can share?

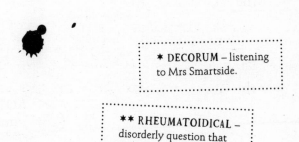

* DECORUM – listening to Mrs Smartside.

** RHEUMATOIDICAL – disorderly question that doesn't have an answer.

CHAPTER 21
INTERNATIONAL TRAVEL NEWS

MRS CHICHESTER AND DAFFODIL CAME
ROUND TODAY FOR SUNDAY TEA,
AND VINNIE TURNED UP TOO.

While Mum and Mrs Chichester drank endless cups of tea in the kitchen, Vinnie took Daffodil and me outside and whispered something about going to his secret den.

'Yorkel,' I said to Vinnie, showing off to Daffodil that we had a secret language – if she feels like she has to compete to be my friend, all the better.

But I stopped as we stepped out of the back door. The pigs had put in a double-whopper full shift on the POOING front.

'Um . . .
Daffodil, your dress
might get dirty,' I said.

'I don't mind,' said Daffodil. 'I hate this dress,
anyway.'

'Really? Why wear it, then?' I asked.

'Oh, my mum likes it,' she said. 'She likes
anything flowery. Dresses, cushions, scented
candles.'

'And you don't?'

'Um, do you have eyes? This stuff is beyond HIDEOUS.'

Well, you could have knocked me over with a bunch of wild daisies. I was *not* expecting her to say *that*.

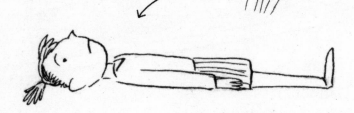

I'm beginning to see that Daffodil has real prospects of dethroning Aleeshaa as my best friend.

And it turns out, although Daffodil is on the fluffy side, she is *not* stupid. For instance, she told me one of the royal family shares my birthday. You see, one of her grandparent's cousins used to be a lady-in-waiting to the queen.

'What's a lady-in-waiting?' I asked.

'It's someone who hangs around all day waiting to do things with the queen,' Daffodil said in her 'royal' voice. She also wants to do some hanging about for the queen when she grows up.

Vinnie led us off to see his secret den – but before we left the farmyard he told us we had to pledge allegiance to the SECRET BOGEY CLUB. Considering he has a very loose grasp of the English language, I wondered out loud where he got the word allegiance from, and he said America – that was a surprise too.

Daffodil was pretty shocked about pledging allegiance to anything to do with BOGEYS, but I told her it's a farming thing.

So this is what Daffodil and I had to do to join **THE BOGEY CLUB**. We had to stick our finger up our nose and then say,

'HMMM . . . NICE BIT OF **BREAKFAST**.'

To my surprise, Daffodil went for it straightaway. I was fine with it too. We hid in the hay shed for a bit to make sure no one was following us before we set off across the fields.

'What's wrong with that lazy horse?' said Daffodil.

'That's High Five,' I said. 'Supposedly he's going to be a great racehorse.'

"'E'S GOT A CHAMPION SIRE,'

said Vinnie, stringing some words together.

'Hmm,' said Daffodil. High Five was sprawling around with Beanstalk and not looking much like a champion.

The den turned out to be an old shed that a shepherd used to use – as did his sheep. Vinnie is tickled PINK with this den.

Daffodil thinks she can probably get some cushions to make it a bit more comfortable, and I said no flowers on them, please, and she laughed. I told her scented candles wouldn't go amiss, though, because this place does have a not-nice niff.

Vinnie produced a packet of squashed-fly biscuits so we sat down on the sheep's droppings and ate them.

SCHOOL NEWS: Daffodil told me stuff about the Lower Goring village school which is quite alarming. It sounds like I shall be tarred and feathered as soon as I set foot in the place. And then strung up over their barbecue and slowly roasted. Apparently there are **FERAL** children all over the place.

Yikes.

Daffodil also let slip that our teacher Miss Bossom 'has *a past*'. Maybe she is on an international wanted list?

I was having such a double-whopper good time with Vinnie and Daffodil that I decided to show them my **MAGIC POCKET WATCH**. But just as I was about to fish it out of its leather belt, there was a breaking-in noise and guess what? Harold had followed us to the secret den and was shouting,

'I know you're in there, losers.'

Before long we'll be steaking out* Lower Goring as our patch and it will be a no-go zone for Harold and **FERAL** children.

> **★ STEAKING OUT** – establishing territory that you control for the purposes of eating and other stuff.

– Daffodil has now overtaken Vinnie
as the front runner to become my
countryside best friend.

PS I have found a very good place to hide the
MAGIC POCKET WATCH at night-time – while
I'm asleep. There is a loose* floorboard under my
bed. No one will ever find it there.

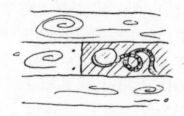

> * **LOOSE** – floorboard that missed
> out on getting any nails.

CHAPTER 22
HOLLY HOPKINSON, PRIVATE INVESTIGATOR

TODAY IS MONDAY, THE DAY DAD IS SUPPOSED TO BE TAKING ME FREELANCING WITH HIM – BUT I'M THINKING OF GRABBING A BIT OF TOAST AND THEN HAVING A LEISURELY LIE-IN. WHICH WILL BE FINE BECAUSE DAD DOESN'T FINISH HIS THINKING TIME AND TV STUFF TILL LUNCHTIME.

But double-whopper flipping well knock me over with the TV controls. There was Dad up for breakfast and wearing a SUIT – he hadn't even turned the TV on.

'Chop chop,** Holly,' Dad said in his 'PERKY' voice. 'We've got a busy day in front of us.'

> ** CHOP CHOP – get your backside into gear.

143

Our first stop was at the library in Chipping Topley. When we got to the car park, Dad explained that we wouldn't be allowed to talk when we were inside.

'What are we actually researching today?' I asked.

Dad looked vacant.* 'Um . . . statistics** . . . for the council . . . very boring . . . you can read a nice book if you like.'

'OK. By the way, Dad, thanks for bringing me. I know you really like doing stuff with Harold usually.'

'And you, Holly,' Dad said in his 'defensive' voice. 'I like doing things with you too.'

Dad gave a glum-looking woman behind the library reception desk a cheery, 'Good morning.'

She looked at him blankly.

I thought, well if you had to spend every day surrounded by books on statistics, you're bound to be a bit **MISBOD**.***

Anyway, we chose our books and started researching. But **double-dealer** Dad seemed to be hiding something under the book he was meant to be looking at.

So I sneaked up and looked over his shoulder and GOTYA.

- ᐟ BUSTINO. ᐟ

He was reading a recipe for cheese soufflé.

What are parents like?

'EXCUSE YOU ...
WHAT ARE YOU READING, DAD?' I asked.

'Just checking the council's menu,' he said, going red, as if he'd done some bottom music.

'Really?' I replied.

145

*** MISBOD – person who would rather be watching racing.

I began to have grave doubts about this whole library carry-on, so I sidled up to the glum woman in reception and fished out my **MAGIC POCKET WATCH**.

She looked pretty strong, so I decided I'd give her a big dose.

'SPIRO, SPERO, SQUIGGLEOUS SCOTCH, CAST YOUR EYES WHITHER MY WATCH!'

I commanded five times, as I waved my **MAGIC WATCH** backwards and forwards in front of her nose.

'Yes?' she said, her eyes now a bit blurry.

'How often does my dad come to this library?' I asked.

'Who?'

'That man over there,' I said, pointing.

'Never seen him in my life,' she said.

'What . . . Are you sure?'

'Positive, young lady . . . now hush . . . you're *not* allowed to disturb people by talking in the library.'

'But there's no one else here to disturb.'

'That's not the point . . . rules are rules.'

'Well, have a nice day,' I replied.

'How can I? No one reads books any more.'

I think I might have overcooked her a bit!

Huh.

Dad is now on my NAUGHTY list. But I decided to play cool with him for now.

Then Dad said he had to meet someone from the council for our next point of business – at the Chequers.

NEWS FLASH: As you know I was under the strict impression that the Chequers is a business centre, but as it turns out – and you WILL BE SHOCKED BY THIS DOUBLE-WHOPPER NEWS – the Chequers is not a business centre – it's a flipping PUB.

No kidding – the place is a SHAMBLES – it's got sawdust on the floor and some rubbish music playing and people who look like they're glued to their seats. And, come to think of it, it smells like Dad does when he comes back from his rural freelancing meetings.

Once I'd recovered from this monumental shock, I saw a noticeboard with lots of things pinned to it. One poster caught my eye.

I think Harold will be most interested to hear that our village hosts a bona fide *music venue*. A little bird was telling me this could be somewhere to play his new songs. Or maybe just one new song that he happened to write on my birthday, perhaps. Which he could loudly dedicate to me so all the kids in the village can hear; and that will really BIG ME UP.

This could be his big break – and, naturally, I also have my royalties to think about!

Garfield, the man 'from the council', was waiting for us at a table, with a large glass of beer in his hand. While Dad went to the bar, I got my MAGIC POCKET WATCH out spit-spot.

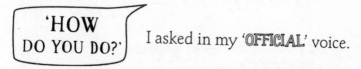 'HOW DO YOU DO?' I asked in my 'OFFICIAL' voice.

'Not bad, man,' he replied. Although there must be something seriously wrong with him if he thinks I'm a man.

On that evidence I decided that Garfield might be made from similar material as Vinnie. So I only gave him two verses of SPIRO, SPERO.

'Do you work for the council?' I asked.

'No.'

'Well, who *do* you work for?'

'The butcher in Chipping Topley.'

'The butcher . . . what are you doing here, then?'

'Having a spot of lunch with your dad . . . and a chat about cricket . . . your dad is **mad** about it.'

Dad has **never** told me he likes cricket.

'Are you sure we are talking about the same George Hopkinson?'

'He loves it, man . . . and I'm named after one of his favourite players . . . Sir Garfield Sobers.'

This was a teacup in a storm I HAD **NOT** been expecting.

'Well, Sir Garfield . . . I'm going to have to excuse you . . . cos Dad's got some explaining to do . . . and he will *not* be discussing butchery or cricket or a combo of the two this lunchtime . . . thank you very much. *Adios.*'

And off Sir Garfield popped. I am *nailing* this MAGIC lark.

'Where's Garfield?' Dad asked when he got back with our drinks.

'He's gone back to the butcher's, Dad . . . So now you and I are going to have a little chat about this "freelancing" of yours,' I said.

WHO SAYS IT'S EASY BEING A

TEN-YEAR-OLD?

CHAPTER 23

DICK WHITTINGTON RETURNS

MY CHAT WITH DAD **WASN'T EASY**,
BUT I THINK HE UNDERSTANDS
WHERE I'M COMING FROM.

I do not expect him to be perfect – but he is my parent and I *only* have *two* of them – so they need to act the part a *bit*.

In the end he came clean with me. His rural freelancing work has hit the fan – vamoosed – CRASHED and **BURNED** – SCARPOED – and he's been kidding all of us that it had continued.

'Never mind that, Dad,' I said in my 'grown-up' voice. 'But what would you *really* like to do now to earn us some money?'

Check this out – he only wants to be a DOUBLE-WHOPPER flipping **chef**. Well, I wasn't expecting that, thank you very much.

'ERM, YOU **CAN'T** COOK, DAD,'

I said.

'I THOUGHT VERA COULD GIVE ME SOME LESSONS ... AND I COULD STUDY IN THE LIBRARY.'

'Dad, I'm not sure Vera is your best bet. That birthday cake she made could have wiped out the entire population of Chipping Topley if someone had dropped it from an aeroplane.

There must be someone else who can help you?'

I thought it best to pretend that I hadn't noticed the TV cookery screen-time abuse.

'I don't know. It's a pretty big career change – maybe it's silly?' he said, looking sad.

Then I had a *brilliant* idea.

BOOM.

'Dad, you've got to enter the CAKE-OFF at the village fete. Lots of people will be there . . . if you WIN that, everyone will want you to cook for them . . . that'll launch your new career.'

Dad looked doubtful. 'Well, I'm not cooking for that Mrs Smartside or Charmain Chichester,' he replied in his 'Harold' voice.

So I gave him a straight talking-to about not being too selective about which chickens he's going to cook that he doesn't have.

And he'll flipping well have to keep watching the daytime TV nonsense.

HOLLY HOPKINSON IS

COOKING ON GAS.*

* COOKING ON GAS –
red hot. But not very green.

154

VERY BIG BREAKING NEWS –

Mum's only doing the PR for the queen's garden party at Buckingham Palace. It's not for ages, but as Mum says, it *does not* get any bigger than that.

It's a big CHEESE deal to throw a party for all those gardeners. And there will be the ladies-in-waiting hanging about looking for the queen and scoffing all the egg sandwiches, I'll bet. As if gardeners aren't a greedy lot, themselves.

'Does that mean you'll meet the queen?'

'Well, I'll be working with *her* people. And apparently she's very hands-on.'

'No, not the gardening . . . honestly, Holly, I sometimes wonder where your head is.'

Well, she's a fine one to talk, but I gave Mum some high fives and a special CUDDLE because she looked so pleased anyway. Organising big parties like this could be the answer for the future of the currently impoverished Hopkinson family. We might even be able to buy Grandpa some more fencing for his chickens.

Or move back to London, and leave the flipping chickens to fight their own corner.

PS When Mum was saying goodnight just now, my MAGIC POCKET WATCH and I had a *good* idea. As I've recently decided that Daffodil should really be my numero uno *best friend* while we're still stuck in the countryside, I should cement the deal by taking her to London to meet the queen, who she is OBSESSED with.

So, I gave Mum three doses of **SPIRO, SPERO**.

'That's a lovely watch, Holly,' she said in a '**GOGGLE-EYED**' voice.

'You will **forget** you've ever seen it, Mum.'

'Yes, Holly.'

'Do you have a meeting at Buckingham Palace soon with the queen's people?'

'As a matter of fact I do, in a couple of days' time.'

'EXCELLENT, MUM ... YOU WILL TAKE ME AND DAFFODIL WITH YOU.'

'Certainly, Holly.'

'Thanks, Mum.'

PPS I also got Mum to text Aleeshaa's mum to see if Aleeshaa would like to meet us at Buckingham Palace.

DICK WHITTINGTON RETURNS –
THE BELLS WILL BE RINGING WHEN
DAFFODIL AND I APPROACH THE CITY.

CHAPTER 24

THE ROYAL SOCIETY OF YOUNG GARDENERS

I WAS SO EXCITED I THOUGHT MY EARS
WOULD **BLOW OFF.** TAKING DAFFODIL
TO BUCKINGHAM PALACE WAS GOING TO
GUARANTEE BFF STATUS. AND WOULD MEAN
STARTING SCHOOL WITH AN INFLUENTIAL
FRIEND ALREADY IN THE BAG.

Aunt Electra was right about the **MAGIC** lasting
as long as it needed to. Two days after my bedtime
cuddle with Mum, she was taking me and Daffodil
to London. I think she was not-so-secretly
pleased to tell Mrs Chichester where we were
going.

The train was packed but there was no fooling
around in the buffet car with people picking each
other up.

When we got there, I was hoping Daffodil would be all over-excited and wanting to pump me for info – like when you can jump on and off buses – and why they drive around two at a time – and why taxis don't stop if their light isn't on – as she'd never had a day out in London with a mate before – but she seemed to be dead cool about it all.

BAD NEWS: when we got to the back door of Buckingham Palace, there was no sign of Aleeshaa anywhere.

'**WHERE IS SHE?**' I asked Mum.

'It was very short notice,' Mum replied in her 'it's-not-the-end-of-the-world' voice.

Well, it may not have been for Mum, but it was a massive slap in the face with a wet HADDOCK for me.

Anyway, Mum arranged to leave me and Daffodil in a waiting room while she had her meeting. Then we were going to find some bread to feed the ducks in St James's Park. ←

(WHICH WAS HARDLY GOING TO RESCUE MY URBAN COOL WITH DAFFODIL, WAS IT?)

'My mum must think I'm simple if she thinks I'm coming all the way to London to feed ducks,' I told Daffodil, trying to sound RISKY. 'We're going to see the queen.'

'What? How?' Daffodil asked. Finally I had her proper attention.

'Just leave that to me,' I said boldly.

One of the queen's great big guardsmen wearing a big black bear's hat was standing guard next to a door which had a sign on it saying, PRIVATE.

So I told Daffodil to hang back. She gave me a funny look, but wandered fake-casually a bit further away while I approached the guardsman.

I pulled out my MAGIC POCKET WATCH and gave him three verses.

'Clear off,' he barked.

161

Knickers, I thought. He'll have to have the works. So I gave him six more verses and he went all SQUIFFY-EYED.

'Please take us to the queen this minute,' I requested in my 'royal' voice. 'You can announce me and my associate* here –' I beckoned Daffodil over as I quickly pocketed the watch – 'as the DIRECTORS OF THE ROYAL SOCIETY OF YOUNG GARDENERS.'

'Yes, miss,' he obeyed.

Phew. We were **in**.

* ASSOCIATE – sounds more official than 'classmate'.

CHAPTER 25

ROYAL APPROVAL

'BUT, HOLLY, I DON'T KNOW
ANYTHING ABOUT GARDENING,'
DAFFODIL PROTESTED AS SHE JOINED ME.

'Don't worry, the queen isn't very hands-on when it comes to gardening – I checked. She probably hasn't dug up any potatoes for years.'

We scuttled along a rather dusty corridor – past a table with a half-empty bowl of Bombay mix on it – until we came to *another* door which said PRIVATE.

The guard officially handed us over to a footman with a very long face and doleful eyes.

'One other thing,' I said to the bear soldier. 'If I have any more trouble with my brother and sister, will you come and deal with them?'

'Yes, miss,' he said. 'Be delighted.' (So that's what's coming your way if you read my memoirs, you two.)

'Can I help?' said the footman in a very 'unhelpful' voice. (He did have big feet, so that's obviously how he got that job.)

FOOTMAN

'They're from the ROYAL SOCIETY OF YOUNG GARDENERS to see the queen,' our bear-soldier told the footman before he marched off.

When the footman opened the door to the queen's sitting room, the first thing we saw was a lady in a light blue headscarf and matching coat dancing slowly round the TV with four corgis barking their heads off.

'RUN, YOU BRUTE, RUN,' she shouted.

'That's how Grandpa behaves when he's watching the racing,' I said to Daffodil.

'Oh, bother,' the lady then said. 'One's horse has just run like a **HAIRY GOAT**. I just don't know what one's trainers do with one's horses sometimes.'

'Excuse you, but my grandpa knows a lot about racing,' I said, realising this was *the queen*. and quickly adding, 'Your Majesty,' in case she reverted* to her ancestors' nasty habit of cutting heads off.

* REVERTED – goes backwards, either in a car or time.

165

'Oh, really . . . well, your grandpa must come and look round the stud at Sandringham one day,' said the queen.

'Thank you, ma'am,' Daffodil said, doing a **massive** curtsy. (Which really showed me up. She could have warned me about that prototype* stuff.)

'They're from the Royal Society of Young Gardeners,' a large butler-type man dressed as a penguin reminded the queen. Not that anyone was asking him, thank you very much.

His stomach looked as if he'd swallowed one of Vera's chocolate cakes without cutting it into slices, he had a muffin stuffed inside each cheek and his mouth resembled an economy-sized macaroon.

* PROTOTYPE –
designing good manners.

'I think they're your eldest son's lot,' he then haughtily snorted.

'What can I offer you ladies to drink? Gardening is such thirsty work,' the queen asked, ignoring the stuffy penguin.

'A CUP OF STRONG TEA WITH SO MUCH SUGAR THE SPOON STANDS UP, PLEASE.'

requested Daffodil, doing another bowing-type manoeuvre.

'What?' I whispered.

'It's what our gardener drinks,' Daffodil said. 'Trust me.'

'Er, me too, please, ma'am,'** I said.

'What was it that you wanted, by the way?' the queen asked.

'Oh, we just wanted to make sure the arrangements for our garden party were coming along OK,' I replied.

** MA'AM – luckily Daffodil told me you pronounce ma'am like jam.

'Yes, everything's fine . . . we've got the American ambassador coming, the prime minister and a man from Cornwall who makes organic cheese.'

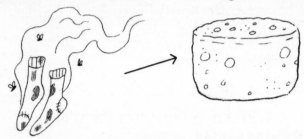

'That will be another one of his lot,' the butler muttered under his breath. 'They probably make it using local SOCKS.'

'Well, one must go,' the queen said. 'One's got another runner in the next race . . . he's called One's for the Road.'

'I see it's shortened from six to one to four to one,' I observed, looking at the odds on the TV.

'Yes . . . one has had a little interest . . . anything else?'

'I don't suppose you've got a horse that my grandpa could follow the next time it runs, have you? A **tip** for him, as it were?'

Obviously I could have whipped out my **MAGIC POCKET WATCH**, but if you get caught doing stuff like that to the queen, you get to have your head displayed on a **spike** outside the Tower of London, thank you very much!

'Well,' the queen said. 'One's got a nice colt by Royal Approval called **Fist Bump** . . . don't ask me how the grandchildren came up with that name. But if one's trainer has pulled his finger out, it should bolt up. One might even have the crown jewels on it.'

BINGO.

GET IN THERE –

Grandpa is going to LOVE me when I get home!

HOLY MOLY – it turns out that Grandpa's lazy foal High Five will have a famous **brother** if ma'am is right about **Fist Bump** winning.

(FOR THOSE OF YOU **NOT** CONCENTRATING, HIGH FIVE AND FIST BUMP HAVE THE SAME **DAD**. THERE CAN'T BE **TWO** HORSES CALLED ROYAL APPROVAL.)

169

And in the world of racing, as every Racing Associate knows, that means High Five's value is going to go through the roof; *and* I've also got a HOT TIP from ma'am for Grandpa, which will mean *pay day*.

Grandpa might turn out to be right about trading his cows for High Five, after all.

WHOOP!

CHAPTER 26

BACK TO THE DIVING BOARD

TALK ABOUT BACK TO THE **SMELLY** COUNTRYSIDE AFTER THE GLAMOUR OF THE PALACE WITH A FLIPPING **BUMP.**

And school is about to start.

This is Holly Hopkinson's **DARKEST** hour

There is only one small bright side to this *doom* and *gloom*: Mum cancelled all her fancy gardeners' meetings this afternoon and came back to the farm to hang out with me. She's pulled a stunt like that before for Harmony, but never with me. So I'm pretty double-whopper flipping pleased about this.

The first thing I wanted to do with her was cook some pancakes. Bad choice. Flipping is not something that PR gurus should try on their afternoons off – the pancakes ended up everywhere, including on Beanstalk, who was bang in the way where Mum couldn't see her.

Then Harmony showed up and was jealous that I'd been having a good time with Mum and tried to make me clear up the flipping MESS – as if she double-whopper cares about stuff like that –

I DON'T THINK SO.

So *Mum and* I retreated to the Bedouin tent and chilled out. Mum asked me if I was worried about my new school, and I said it has been getting mixed reviews in my head. Sometimes using MUM SPEAK is the only way to get through to her.

Then we did some reading. And considering my mum has become a guru I am a bit surprised by the quality of – or should I say lack of – her reading material.

Then Mum asked me if I was happy living on the farm, but I told her I wasn't in the mood to do games with lots of questions. So she smiled and gave me a KISS.

Mum says that Harmony and Harold are both a bit worried about their new schools too, so for the first time in history we're on the same page. The Hopkinson offspring will be coming face to face with a new world tomorrow – some of us may not survive it; my money's on Harold CROAKING it. Harmony will just chain herself to some railings if it all gets a bit tough.

Then Dad made us crumpets, which he toasted on an open fire outside the kitchen. He said he's going to build a pizza oven and maybe start a take-away business. Mum thinks the 'walk-in' trade might be limited, but Dad reckons we could all deliver them on bicycles. I think he needs to go back to the diving board with *that* business plan, thank you very much.

Grandpa and I spent some time after tea leaning on the gate watching High Five gallop round the field, with Beanstalk hot on his tail. Grandpa was double-whopper excited to find out that the q\ueen has one of High Five's brothers – who is going to *win* a race very soon.

'I KNEW I'D PICKED A GOOD'UN,'

Grandpa said.

CHAPTER 27

OFFICIALLY A LAUGHING STOCK

THE MOMENTOUS DAY HAS COME.

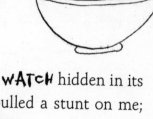

My legs were in a very reluctant mood as I stepped off the school bus, and my boots felt like they were wading through a bowl of Vera's suet pudding.

I had my **MAGIC POCKET WATCH** hidden in its special belt in case anyone pulled a stunt on me; although I still felt pretty **NERVY**.

And, sure enough, the village school is a weird place. To start with they don't have any security on the front door. Literally **anyone** could just walk in and kidnap us.

175

I've read about that in the papers. Someone puts up a huge ransom and, knowing my luck, Barkley will eat the ransom note and that will be the tragic end of my writing career. So if this comes to a grinding halt, you'll know my parents didn't get the note. Or if they did, they didn't pay up!

Then there's the playground. It hasn't got a NET above it. So anything could fall out of the sky and land on our heads – including bird poo or someone flushing the BOG on an aeroplane.

(HAVE YOU EVER THOUGHT WHERE THAT ENDS UP?)

And the playground is just grass and mud, and there's no tarmac and paint to show you where it's safe to play. It's SCANDALOUS, really.

Daffodil is kind of in 'Mrs Chichester's-perfect-daughter mode', but she says she's watching my back. She also warns me to look out for any mice hiding in the BOGS. I hope she is joking.

Three girls called Iris, Crocus and Amaryllis are in my class. When I told Dad their names, he said the local garden centre must have had some sort of promotion going on when they were born.

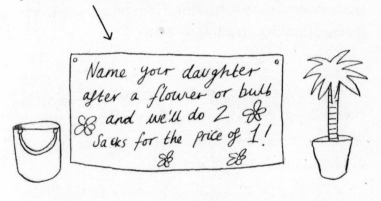

Name your daughter after a flower or bulb and we'll do 2 sacks for the price of 1!

Anyway, they can all talk the hind legs off a donkey. Especially Crocus – it's like being at a parrot convention on National Squawking Day, thank you very much.

But they are not FERAL at all. In fact, I'm beginning to wonder whether Daffodil has just been winding me up like Dad does with Harmony.

There is, *however*, Felicity Snoop. And someone has tipped me off that she used to be Daffodil's best friend, so I might have a bit of a fight on my hands there.

Then there are three boys that sit at the back of the classroom – Gaspar, Tiger and Wolfe. Dad says the vicar must have thought he was working at the flipping local ZOO when he christened them!

Anyway, they were showing off and bigging themselves up a lot on my first morning, which was cute – let's hope they *stay* cute. The boys at my London school *did not*.

And then there was another boy called Brian, who was dressed for cricket, which was a bit STRANGE as no one's told me we're going to be playing cricket.

'HOW DO YOU DO?' I said by way of introduction to Brian in my 'formal' voice.

'Not bad . . . not bad,' he replied. So I don't know what's the matter with him.

AKA **BOSSY BOSSOM**, BOTTY BOSSOM
AND **BIG BOSSOM** ↘

My teacher is called Miss Bossom, as you already know. She used to be an actress – Daffodil says she still is when she gets going.

The first thing Miss Bossom wanted to teach us about was the Christmas show that we're going to do. She went floating around the classroom twirling her skirt and saying,

'**OH, THE FOOTLIGHTS**, THE SMELL OF THE **GREASEPAINT**, THE RAUCOUS **APPLAUSE** FROM THE AUDIENCE.'

She clearly **doesn't** get out much.

'The show is called *Cinderella and her Wicked Sisters*,' Miss Bossom announced. 'I've adapted it from the classic tale, and it's rather good.'

'What does "adapted" mean?' I whispered to Daffodil.

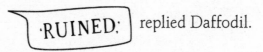 ·RUINED· replied Daffodil.

This does NOT bode well for mending the roof.

Then the bell went for lunch.

Vinnie was hanging around with some other boys outside the lunch hall, so I went up to have a chinwag.

'Hmm . . . Nice bit of breakfast,' I said to Vinnie, sticking my finger up my nose and winking.

The other boys started laughing – and Vinnie went RED and *ignored* me.

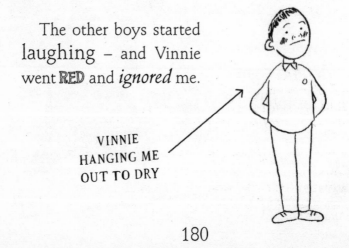

VINNIE
HANGING ME
OUT TO DRY

I felt like a right CHUMP – and I have been *betrayed*. Vinnie will go down in history with Judas Iscariot* and Wayne Rooney** as the biggest traitor ever. Just when I thought I had got my new school career off to a flying start, I am brought crashing to the ground by someone who keeps SNAILS in his pockets.

And, yes, after all that I turned round to see Felicity Snoop sniggering delightedly at me.

I AM OFFICIALLY A

DOUBLE-WHOPPER

LAUGHING STOCK.

* JUDAS ISCARIOT – swapped sides from Jesus to the Romans.

** WAYNE ROONEY – Dad says he swapped bars from Everton to Man Utd and then back.

CHAPTER 28

AN OVERAMBITIOUS VENTURE

WAR-ZONE NEWS –
IT ALL KICKED OFF THIS MORNING –
BIG-STYLE.

As if I didn't have enough trouble at school, now that Vinnie has cast me to the wolves, I also have adult STRIFE at home.

Aunt Electra has made one of her usual unannounced visits. Mum is less than impressed – not least because she's found a poster at the railway station advertising Pilates classes to be held at the farm.

'ARE YOU RESPONSIBLE FOR **THIS?**'

Mum asked Aunt Electra.

'Darling, I thought it would be such fun . . . and make some money for the farm.'

'Well, thank you for asking,' Mum said in her 'UNGRATEFUL' voice.

But I think Mum is right – you can't just go round inviting the world to Pilates classes in other people's houses without asking them.

Sometimes Aunt Electra does push the boat out a bit without legs to stand on.

Then Dad gave us some **SURPRISING NEWS**. He's going to cook supper for the entire family tonight.

Mum said, 'Shall I bring a Chinese takeaway home with me just in case?' which Harold seemed to find very amusing.

'We've got plenty of eggs,' Grandpa reminded Dad. 'And you can't beat Florence's milk at this time of the year . . . full of cream . . . I'll be out to milk her in a JIFFY.'

'I'm, like, a vegan,'* pointed out Harmony.

183

* VEGAN – bolshy teenager who persecutes nuts.

'No, you're not,' snapped Mum. 'And dinner tonight is not about you.'

Harmony looked furious, absolutely furious that her BESTIE Mum had criticised her – but I was rather pleased.

'Well, spit-spot,' whooshed Dad. 'Off to school and London, you lot. I need peace and quiet in my kitchen. We haven't got all day.'

'But you have,' Mum pointed out. 'What are you going to cook us?'

'Er . . . it depends what they're doing today.'

'They?'

'LET'S KEEP IT AS A SURPRISE,'

I said quickly. I know exactly who *they* are – the chefs on TV.

Harmony has gone to the limit with her uniform.

'Ready for St Trinian's?' asked Dad. He should know by now that the school is called St Margaret's.

Unbelievably Harold has already made a friend there called Stickly – they're thinking about forming a band. So I have suggested that they will need a manager, and I am happy to offer Holly Hopkinson BAND MANAGER INC's services. Harold has officially accepted my terms.

I had a **BAD** feeling about Dad's dinner at school all day. I ignored Vinnie ignoring me and couldn't even concentrate on a game of Double Dutch* that Daffodil wanted me to join in with the other flowers.

What if Dad POISONED all of us? The police and TV cameras that they always bring with them would think it was a mass killing. The Hopkinson family would finally be famous, but not for a good reason.

HERE LIES
HOLLY HOPKINSON
WHO HAD
SECONDS

* DOUBLE DUTCH –
posh country kids game.

Meanwhile, Miss Bossom made us start auditing* for her Christmas show – *Cinderella and her whatevers*. I told her that we have chickens on the farm if she needs any eggs for the stage decoration. Just being helpful, of course, not sucking up for a good part.

My heart sank even further when the school bus driver dropped me off at the top of the lane. They were the first blue flashing lights that I'd seen since London.

Although this time it was a fire engine, not a police van . . .

And it was parked right outside our house.

*AUDITING – counting other people get the parts.

CHAPTER 29

WHAT WENT WRONG WITH DINNER?

SO THIS IS THE
UP-TO-DATE BREAKING NEWS
THAT I'VE BEEN ABLE TO PIECE TOGETHER
FROM THE EYE-WITNESS ACCOUNTS OF
VERA, GRANDPA AND DAD, AND FROM SEEING
BEANSTALK, WHO WAS IN A RIGHT STATE.

Dad said he turned the TV on to see what they were cooking that morning – then Vera turned up 'and started being a pest'.

Vera said Dad was making a terrible MESS and the people in the TV shows are idiots – so he was doing it the wrong way; and she was just trying to help.

Grandpa said no one told him to use the saucepan and not a wine glass when he was asked to help reduce the red wine. And it wasn't his fault that he was left with Beanstalk watching the CHIP PAN while Dad popped into Chipping Topley to get some self-raising flour.

Vera said if it wasn't for her the whole place would have gone up in flames – she knew that the fire extinguishers were all empty, so she called the fire brigade.

'Why are they empty?' I asked Vera.

'Because your grandpa is on the breadline . . . not that you lot coming here has helped.'

Well, I wasn't taking that standing still. So I asked her what his diet has got to do with us. And she just rolled her eyes at me and made a Northern noise.

Anyway, the firemen said the Chinese takeaway was nice. Luckily Mum bought far too much *as usual*.

Apparently Aunt Electra just rushed about SCREAMING when the fire started, and then swanned around the firemen until she got bored and disappeared back to Bohemia without anyone really noticing.

Mum said, 'She couldn't stand the HEAT so she got out of the kitchen.'

Dad said, 'Bit close to the bone, that one.'

Then Mum dropped a double-whopper **fully explosive BOMBSHELL**.

'Of course, Aunt Electra this and Aunt Electra that is all NONSENSE,' she declared.

Dad pulled a face like he knew he was about to sit on a drawing pin.

189

'SHE IS **ACTUALLY** CALLED ETHEL.'

Dad sighed.

'Excuse you . . . backup there, if you please . . .
What do you mean she's actually called Ethel?' I
asked.

'That's her real name.'

'Is that true, Dad?'

Dad gave a sheepish nod like Barkley does after
he's said cheeky things to the poodle in the park.

'Well, poor Aunt Electra being made to change
her name by the bohemians,' I said in my
'**LOYAL**' voice.

(I THINK WE'LL BRUSH ETHEL
UNDER THE CARPET – NOT COOL.)

Mum and Dad called a family **CRISIS** meeting
with Harold, Harmony and me.

We have all agreed that if the Hopkinson family
are to make it through to the next century, we all
need to pull together.

Before we went to bed, Harmony let me go up to her room for the first time ever and she showed me a few of her things – she has TOP SECRET pictures of her favourite singer wearing trousers that are twelve centimetres too short for him and cradling his guitar. He thinks he looks cool, which is a terrific laugh.

So the day wasn't a *total* disaster.

For once.

CHAPTER 30

THE MYSTERY BOX

MUM HAS GOT A PR *DISASTER* LOOMING AND SHE'S 'FIGHTING FIRES ON TWO FRONTS' ACCORDING TO HER COVERT* TELEPHONE CONVERSATION WITH ONE OF THE FETE COMMITTEE, WHICH I JUST HAPPENED TO OVERHEAR FROM BEHIND THE SOFA.

FIRST PROBLEM – Harmony is threatening to hold a demonstration at the entrance to the fete to highlight inequality.**

'Harmony, what has inequality got to do with the village fete? Have you *already* forgotten that we're meant to be pulling together?' Mum has been asking.

---

* COVERT – sneaky beaky.

** INEQUALITY – difference between a bloke carrying a girl, and a bloke carrying a bloke

Harmony says the rules of the Tough Farmer competition 'give the impression that the female farmers and their boyfriends or girlfriends, or pets for that matter, can't enter.'

Dad says Harmony should be an ambulance-chasing lawyer when she grows up; or –

even worse –

a High Court judge. ⟶

ORDER!

SECOND PROBLEM – I think Mum might have over-promised on delivering a celebrity to open the fete.

'Her people' had a motoring TV star and a guitarist from a famous band who both live near Chipping Topley in mind (top secret – no names), but *neither* of *their* people will answer *their* phones.

Anyway, they're now having an emergency fete committee meeting. And I've made sure that I'm here handing out the biscuits. ☺

ITEM ONE – Harmony's Protest. Mum reassured the committee that she's going to pay Harmony off.

ITEM TWO – Distinct lack of celebrity news, but Mrs Smartside said she will save the day and open the fete if need be.

ITEM THREE – Programme of Events for the main arena – **TOP SECRET**:

2.00pm – Grand Opening

2.30pm – Tough Farmer Challenge

3.00pm – Ferret racing with a difference. Vince says the winner is the first person who can get a ferret to go up one trouser leg and come out of the other.

3.30pm – Mud-wrestling

4.00pm – The Big Fat Cake-off. This is obviously the big one. **UNDER-THE-RADAR NEWS** – Dad is getting cold feet,* but don't worry about that. I've put in an official entry form for him and my **MAGIC POCKET WATCH** will sort out his last-minute nerves.

* **COLD FEET** – what you get if you stand around long enough trying to make your mind up.

Harold and I are going to do a joint stall in the new Hopkinson-family-pull-together 'once more to the beach, dear friend, once more' spirit. That is if I can persuade him to take his headphones off for five seconds.

It's called 'THE MYSTERY BOX'. Basically what you have to do is put your hand through a hole into a big box – then Harold and I put an item into the box from the back and you have to guess what it is. Fifty pence a go – if you guess right, you get another go for free. (**NO SMELLING ALLOWED.**)

Things we have in mind to put in the box include:

A DUCKLING.

TRAIN TICKET.

ROTTEN APPLES.

GRANDPA'S PANTS.

SOMETHING FROM VERA'S FRIDGE.

A FROG.

BEANSTALK.

COW-POO BRICK.

UNBELIEVABLY LATE
OFFICIAL BREAKING NEWS

– Aunt Electra has arrived a day early for the village fete. And she's brought her fortune-telling tent with her. Mum says she doesn't know whether to laugh or cry.

CHAPTER 31

LIKE A BARNACLE ON THE BACKSIDE OF A KILLER WHALE

DAD WAS BEHAVING LIKE A CAT IN A HOT TIN CAN AT BREAKFAST, SO I ASKED HIM TO COME OUTSIDE AND HELP ME COLLECT THE EGGS. WHEN WE WERE IN THE BARN, I GOT MY MAGIC POCKET WATCH OUT AND WHIZZED IT BACKWARDS AND FORWARDS IN FRONT OF HIS NOSE.

'SPIRO, SPERO, SQUIGGLEOUS SCOTCH, CAST YOUR EYES WHITHER MY WATCH.'

I said for his usual dose of three verses.

'What's that all about?' Dad asked.

'Just a game,' I said in my 'CUTE' voice. 'Now, Dad, you will take part in the Cake-off?'

'YES, HOLLY.'

'And you will win . . . all you have to do is concentrate and be focused . . . don't let anything distract you and you will be fine.'

'YES, HOLLY.'

Before we set off to the fete I checked with Mum that she had rung Aleeshaa's mother to invite her.

'Er . . . yes . . . well, they weren't sure if they could make it,' Mum replied. So basically Aleeshaa has abandoned me. *Again.*

Mum was behaving like she'd had too much sugar by the time the Grand Opening Ceremony was due. '*Her* people' had heard that the top-secret famous TV car celebrity might be in the area after all – he'd been spotted buying a burger and fizzy drinks in Chipping Topley that morning – but there was still no sign of him so, 'Without further ado I declare this fete *open*,' gushed Mrs Smartside.

The **FIRST BIG NEWS OF THE DAY** was that they're short of entries for the Tough Farmer competition.

'It's all the meddling what's gone on that's put everyone off,' explained Vince. But this is the funny bit – Harmony has got roped into doing it with Harold's new mate, Stickly.

They'll have to stack bales, make a sheep pen, carry beer barrels and then Stickly has to sink a pint of beer before carrying Harmony back down the course and throwing her into the sheep pen.

(SINCE HE IS UNDERAGE HE WILL BE GIVEN GINGER BEER.)

Dad and I nearly died laughing while we watched them – they lost too.

Sir Garfield, Dad's butcher friend, was one of ten entrants for the ferret racing. He was wearing very baggy cricket trousers, so he must have done this before. Unlike Stickly, who entered the ferret race wearing skinny jeans – he is a double-whopper DOOFUS.

I am pleased to report that things didn't go according to plan for Vinnie in the ferret race, and he ended up in the St John's ambulance tent.

The crowd roared their heads off for Sir Garfield, who won by a leg.

(SCHOOL NEWS – SIR GARFIELD'S GRANDSON IS BRIAN FROM THE BACK ROW OF MY CLASS.)

The mud-wrestling was late for two reasons:

Lack of water – the vicar got the wrong attachment for the extra-long hose that he'd acquired, so he had to carry it in buckets.

The paddling pool the vicar was using had a hole in it from last year and needed mending – something to do with when the Over Sixty-fives' class got OUT OF HAND.

Grandpa won the mud-wrestling class for people with beards. He looked a right state by the time he'd finished. It made him very thirsty too, so he nipped off to the Chequers to have a drink before the Big Fat Cake-off.

Practically squillions of people were having a go on all the stalls, and my best friend Daffodil officially helped me and Harold with THE MYSTERY BOX.

Then guess who thought he could come over and be besties with me and Daffodil? Traitor Vinnie.

'EXCUSE YOU ... CAN I HELP YOU ... WHOEVER YOU ARE,' I asked him.

Vinnie stuck his finger up his nose and timidly said, 'Nice bit of breakfast.'

'Oh, is it?' I asked. 'Well, just so you know we've changed the password, and we've voted you out of the club.'

Vinnie made noises that sounded like words coming out back to front. But after he eventually wandered off Daffodil told me I was right to be tough with him.

I bought one of Vera's cakes off the cake stall and put it in the Mystery Box. Someone guessed it was a CANNON BALL.

We let them have another go, because technically they could be right. Mrs Smartside also had a go at the Mystery Box and it didn't go well. Beanstalk bit her hand, and was then banned from the fete.

Then Daffodil spotted something for the websites and *newspaper* front pages. Miss Bossom arriving at the fete with – guess who – Slinky Dave, the school bus driver. We call him Slinky Dave because he slinks around a lot. Anyway, them arriving together is a bit of scandal.

I'm hoping to land the part of Cinders in the play, so I put a soft, cuddly duckling in the Mystery Box for Big Bossom. She didn't guess right, even though it was making disgruntled quacking noises.

Iris, Crocus and Amaryllis didn't dare do the Mystery Box – they just fluttered around chattering like finches.

Felicity Snoop slithered about, darting NASTY looks at me. And she stuck to Miss Bossom like a barnacle on the backside of a killer whale – she's totally up to something. She is on MAGIC POCKET WATCH borrowed time.

Guess who else turned up?

Ms Growler, the head teacher. Wearing the same long tweed skirt that she wears every day at school.

She moved around like a blinking tortoise on a very bright summer's day and didn't spend any money, I noticed. Tortoises probably don't worry about having a roof over their heads when it rains; they've got their own flipping shells. And Botty Bossom and Slinky Dave kept well away from her, hiding like squirrels round the back of trees.

And then I had to SPIT-SPOT shoot off to the fortune-telling tent and be Aunt Electra's wingman, as she put it. I can't say I'm proud of my role – I was watching who came to the tent and giving Aunt Electra secret inside information on them.

First fool up was Miss Bossom – I told Aunt Electra she was my teacher and she was about to make a right MESS of our Christmas show.

So when Bossy Bossom went into the tent, Aunt Electra started rubbing her glass ball and making SPOOKY noises – and then she said,

'I SEE GREAT THEATRICAL SUCCESS COMING YOUR WAY.'

And Bossy lapped it up and started saying, 'Oh yes, my *Cinderella* adaptation.'

And Aunt Electra went, 'Yes, well, it might be Cinderella or it might not be – she's just gone behind a cloud.' You couldn't make it up.

Then you'll never guess who was next up – I thought she had more sense – Mrs Chichester.

I tipped Aunt Electra off and then she did all the moaning stuff again and said, 'I can see a barn in a farmyard full of cushions – and lots of customers queuing up.'

And Mrs Chichester said, 'WELL, I HAVE BEEN THINKING OF EXPANDING.'

Soon it was time for the Hopkinson family to retire for some lunch. Little did I know, though, that there was going to be *high drama* at the Chequers. And in the BOGS, of all places.

PS Aleeshaa didn't turn up – either she has found a new London best friend or my mother is **not** a very good messenger who's been shot.

CHAPTER 32
A BIT OF BOTTOM MUSIC

GRANDPA HAD SPENT AN HOUR OR SO KEEPING US A TABLE IN THE CHEQUERS FOR LUNCH – IT'S HARDER TO GET A TABLE THERE ON FETE DAY THAN THE 'FLIPPING RITZ', ACCORDING TO MUM.

Dad said they could make a fortune if they did food you could eat. But I was **bursting**, so I didn't have time to hang about debating the shelf life of stewed chicken.

And while I was minding my own business on the BOG, guess who arrived in the loos going at it hammer and tongs – Mum and Aunt Electra.

'What *do you* think you're playing at?' Mum was shouting. They obviously didn't know I was in there, so I kept quiet.

'I'm just trying to help.'

'*Help*⸮!' Talking Charmain Chichester into opening up a branch of her ghastly shop in *our* farmyard⸮'

'IT'S NOT YOUR FARMYARD. IT'S GRANDPA'S.' shouted Aunt Electra.

'Well, we do not want Charmain Chichester there, if you please.'

When Mum says if you please, she is *not* actually trying to please. Even *I* know that.

'But don't you get it⸮' said Aunt Electra. 'Grandpa needs the money, and she would be a very good tenant.'

There was a deathly pause. Just as I was about to play a bit of **BOTTOM** music, thank you very much. I had to squeeze everything to keep quiet.

'What do you mean, he needs the money?'

'He's skint, Sally,' Aunt Electra said in a voice I'd never heard before. 'Broke. Bankrupt. Down to his last pair of underpants. But he won't admit it to you, of course.'

And then there was **silence**. Not a squeak out of Mum.

'Is that really true?' Mum asked.

'Yes, Sally,' Aunt Electra said. 'He's too proud to tell anyone. But it's true.'

Another pause.

'But . . . how do *you* know?'

Aunt Electra let out a long sigh. Like a mouse passing **WIND**. 'Look, Sally, I know you think I'm all over the place, and I am really, but he's my dad. I worry about him, that's all.'

'I . . .' said Mum. 'I . . . I have to go.' And I heard the main door of the **BOGS** close as she walked out.

Aunt Electra hung around a bit, sniffing. Finally she did another big sigh and then walked out too.

Sometimes grown-ups can behave in a very ERRATIC fashion!

So, **LATE LUNCHTIME NEWS** – Grandpa's money troubles are the latest THREAT to my survival – and as I'm his partner, I may be liable for his debts.

PS I think the Chequers could do with some air fresheners for the BOGS, which double-whopper WHIFF on the NIFFING front.

CHAPTER 33

THE CAKE OFF

THE BIG FAT CAKE-OFF IS A SERIOUS BUSINESS - IT EVEN HAS AN OFFICIAL SPONSOR - SCOOBY'S, THE LOCAL PET-FOOD WAREHOUSE.

VILLAGE FETE
CAKE-OFF RULES:

★ Contestants' lemon and carrot cakes will be removed from the oven (heat 175°C) one hour after the start of the competition.

★ Contestants may only use the ingredients on the tables provided. (Help yourself before the starting whistle blows.)

★ Contestants must choose which size baking dish to use (choice of four). Max marks can only be won by biggest tin.

★ No cheating.

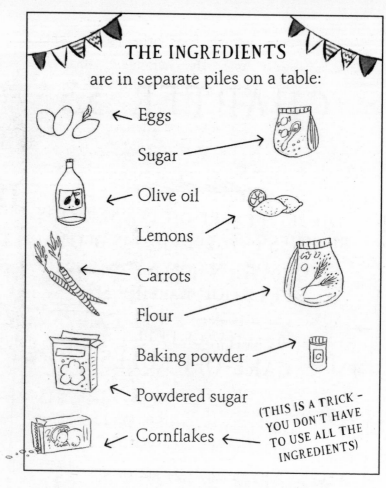

THE INGREDIENTS

are in separate piles on a table:

← Eggs

Sugar →

← Olive oil

Lemons →

← Carrots

Flour →

Baking powder →

← Powdered sugar

Cornflakes ←

(THIS IS A TRICK –
YOU DON'T HAVE
TO USE ALL THE
INGREDIENTS)

So I could see the **problem** from the start. If you make **too** much cake mixture, or take **too** much time making the mixture, it won't cook in time. TRICKY.

There was **no way** Dad was going to figure that out.

He was up against four other contestants. Grandpa, who was the official Cake-off bookmaker, priced them all up:

THE VICAR – I had never heard of a vicar being a cook. But the vicar might finally get help from above, now he'd taken that fireman's hat off. **ODDS 8 TO 1.**

MISS BOSSOM. She doesn't teach cooking at school. But she's trying to impress Slinky Dave. **ODDS 3 TO 1.**

SOME FRENCH BLOKE – he runs a restaurant in Chipping Topley. I told Mum to ask Mrs Smartside if professionals are allowed to enter. I was going to get Harmony to protest if he won, because he's French. **ODDS 6 TO 4. FAVOURITE.**

VERA – she's on the committee so she might have inside information. **ODDS 3 TO 1.**

DAD – he was way out of his league here. But he looked unnervingly calm and the **MAGIC POCKET WATCH** is on his side. **ODDS 33 TO 1.**

The Honourable Judge is Mrs Smartside, of course. 'There can be no doubting my impartiality,* and I have a wealth of experience with the W.I.,'** she said to the media.

All the contestants helped themselves to ingredients and then the Hon. Judge blew her whistle, the crowd started roaring and they were off.

You've never heard so much noise – particularly from the Tough Farmers who'd finished off the beer barrels they'd been carrying about. It was too much for the French bloke – he BLEW his gherkin.

---

* IMPARTIALITY – hasn't had a dose of my Magic Pocket Watch.

** W.I. – Women's Incident – they normally happen in town halls.

214

'WHAT A RACKET,' he shouted

– and other French words. 'How can I cook my beautiful food with all this noise? Look, my eggs are getting UPSET.'

Miss Bossom, on the other hand, was *loving* all the attention. 'Oh, it's just like the old days,' she was purring in between cheeky BOGGLE-EYED smiles to Slinky Dave. But she wasn't concentrating and put the cornflakes in – double-whopper **doofus**.

The vicar was walking around like he was doing communion, with his head in the clouds. And he was looking like he was going to use the biggest cake tin. How many people did he think he had to feed – five thousand? Even with God's help, there was **no way** it would cook in time.

Vera, on the other hand, wasn't hanging about. She was up and at it like a CONCRETE mixer on a building site.

Meanwhile, Dad was an oasis of calm. He quietly whisked his sugar and eggs together – then he drizzled* in olive oil and lemon juice. He's good at grating carrots, that's how Beanstalk likes them, and he didn't go NUTS with the flour and the baking powder.

Only Dad went for the half-size baking tin. Which was a gamble – his would have to be the best cake by some way to win, as it was smaller.

Dad was so nervous he couldn't speak while the cakes were baking. Then Mrs Smartside opened the oven, placed the cakes on the table and asked the competitors to take them out of their tins.

The first DISASTER was the vicar's. His literally walked off the table on to the floor. It wasn't even half cooked. He gave a SHEEPISH grin.

* DRIZZLED – TV-speak
for pour slowly on a miserable day.

The other four cakes at least stood their ground.

The Hon. Judge tried a piece of Botty Bossom's offering – and removed a large chunk of carrot covered in cornflakes from her mouth, which she placed on the table. (NOT GOOD.)

Next was Vera's – but the Hon. Judge couldn't get the knife in. Vince was summoned – he has arms like tree trunks – and he carved a bit off, but the game was up for Vera. She'd produced another MISSILE.

The French bloke was next. The Hon. Judge took a slice – it looked beautiful and light and perfect.

But the Hon. Judge's face looked just like she'd sat on a very wet BOG seat when she tasted it.

'No lemon,' she said. 'Oh dear, no lemon?'

The French bloke waved his arms around a lot and said things in French that he might regret when he calms down. Someone who knows a bit of French said he's banned Mrs Smartside from his restaurant in Chipping Topley, which is *hilarious*.

Finally she got to Dad's cake – half the size of the other cakes – and took a bite.

Someone tapped me on the shoulder. It was Mum, looking a bit sad but excited and tense at the same time. She gripped my hand and we both crossed our fingers.

The judge chewed.

Then a big smile appeared on her face and we all ERUPTED –

DAD WAS THE WINNER!

And then it all kicked off as far as the Hopkinson family having any DECORUM is concerned. Mum gave Dad a big kiss – then Harmony of all people joined in, even though it wasn't about her, and gave Dad a hug! Then, can you believe it, Harold started crying and gave Mum a kiss.

Well, I wasn't going to stand there watching my family make a SPECTACLE of themselves, so I joined in – and Grandpa piled in on top, followed by Aunt Electra, who wasn't going to miss out on a DRAMA.

Even Sir Garfield went BONKERS, cheering, 'You've knocked it out of the park, man.'

Mum took Aunt Electra behind the Cake-off tables and I heard her say,

'I'M SO SORRY, ELECTRA, YOU'RE RIGHT. I WAS BEING SELFISH.'

Then Aunt Electra said, 'Don't be silly, Sally. You've been busy with the job and the kids,' and then the two of them were having a LOVE-IN and hugging each other right in front of the vicar, of all people.

DEARY ME!

But Dad's new career is launched,
so this is officially a

DAY OF TRIUMPH

for the Hopkinson family.

CHAPTER 34

A SILK FIST IN AN IRON GLOVE

I WAS HOPING FOR GOOD NEWS AT
SCHOOL TODAY TOO - BOSSY BOSSOM WAS
CASTING CINDERELLA. I MEAN, THE PLAY IS
GOING TO BE RUBBISH, BUT I'M PREPARED
TO PUT MY ARTISTIC PRINCIPLES TO ONE
SIDE IN EXCHANGE FOR A LEAD ROLE.

That, plus I knew that if I got a killer role in the play, my place in the Little Goring social hierarchy would be *sealed*.

In fact, I was so excited I thought I might **EXPLODE** – which meant the whole classroom would look like one of those crime scenes you see in scary films – there'd be bits of me all over the place and detectives shaking their heads wondering if aliens are involved.

Even though I am the new girl, realistically, Daffodil was my only competition – which was why I went out of my way to give Botty Bossom a cuddly duckling in the Mystery Box at the fete.

But I smelled TROUBLE as soon as I arrived at school –

Miss Bossom was distinctly frosty with me and made a remark about blunt carrot graters. She needs to learn to be a good loser. If she wants to behave like an adult and enter competitions, as Mum says, she should 'buck up' when she doesn't win.

Bossom then told us about her play adaptation. Cinderella enters a TV talent show with Buttons, her faithful sidekick, and her wicked stepsisters. But she falls in LOVE with her Prince Charming, who is one of the judges, during the rehearsals.

Cinderella then runs away because she thinks the judge is in love with Buttons.

Eventually Cinderella returns for the final, wins it and lives happily ever after with the TV judge/ Prince Charming. And Buttons ends up having to work as a lawyer for the rest of his life, which Dad will be pleased about.

She then told us that she'd had word from 'THE BEYOND' that the play was going to be a great success – *beyond* Aunt Electra's fake glass ball, I felt like adding.

If you ask me, Bossy's made a bit of a dog's dinner of it. If anyone thinks Cinderella and her flipping sisters are going to put the roof back on the school, they must have had a BANG on the head à la Vinnie.

'Doesn't this adaptation raise all sorts of ethical issues, Miss Bossom?' I asked in my 'POMPOUS' voice.

'Oh, Holly . . . you're so constrained* by middle-class thinking, my dear,' she replied in her 'actress' voice.

'YOU NEED TO LOOSEN UP A BIT.'

223

* CONSTRAINED – too much packaging, like stuff you buy online.

Well, I had no idea our family was middle class – that is good news – although I need to check that with Mum and Dad.*

Felicity Snoop, sitting in the front row as usual, was nodding sycophantically** at every word Botty said, like a hypnotised Barbie doll.

> **BAD CASTING NEWS** – It wasn't long before the bombshells began to drop, like Vera's cakes in the Blitz.

'Felicity, you shall play Cinderella,' Miss Bossom announced. Those words were like a KNIFE to my heart.

ARE YOU KIDDING?

Well, that meant I *had* to be Prince Charming.

'PRINCE CHARMING SHALL BE PLAYED BY VINNIE,' continued Bossy.

Well, that is a complete joke. Vinnie may be many things, but charming isn't one of them.

* Are the Hopkinson family middle class? Mum said, 'Certainly not.' Dad said, 'Of course we are.' My parents are ridiculous.

** SYCOPHANTICALLY – double sucking up.

I was now numb. And I could feel my **MAGIC POCKET WATCH** twitching in my pocket.

'The wicked stepsisters will be Tiger and Wolfe,' was the next news. Miss Bossom clearly thinks she's clever, throwing boys being girls into the mix. Wolfe was so excited he did some of his BOTTOM music.

'The cruel stepmother is a very important figure in the play,' Bossy told us. So, of course, I thought, *Here comes my part*. And then she gave it to Amaryllis?

Just Buttons and the Fairy Godmother left . . . and then it was just Buttons as Iris got the Fairy Godmother role.

Only one of me or Daffodil could get the part of Buttons. *This was going to test our friendship*, I thought. Daffodil had got her hands on her hips and she was pulling her CROSS FACE.

And then the final slight – *Crocus* was playing Buttons.

'Of course, all parts are equally important,' said Miss Bossom, 'and I know Daffodil will be a triumph as the chicken and Holly and Brian as the ducks.'

Since when did *Cinderella* have a duck in it? This is all revenge for Dad winning the Big Fat Cake-off – anyone can see that. I'm going to be roasted by the FERAL kids and have no friends at all at this rate.

At least Daffodil is not pleased, either. I can report that without fear of contraction.*

But then a window of opportunity shone its light on my life.

'I shall sleep on my castings** and pin them up on the noticeboard tomorrow morning,' Bossy Bossom announced as everyone was leaving the class.

** SLEEPING ON CASTINGS – why her noticeboard looks very crumpled!

* CONTRACTION – squashing the truth

226

As Dad says,

'IT'S NEVER OVER UNTIL THE FAT GOALIE HAS LET IT IN THE NET.'

So I fiddled around in my desk until all the other kids had scarpered, and then I wandered casually up to Botty's desk, quietly swinging my MAGIC POCKET WATCH.

CHAPTER 35

I DON'T EVEN LOOK LIKE A DUCK

'WHAT CAN I DO FOR YOU, HOLLY?'
BOTTY BOSSOM ASKED,
RAISING HER EYEBROWS.

'Look at my MAGIC POCKET WATCH, Miss Bossom,' I said with a cute smile on my face.

'Very nice, Holly . . . how interesting,' she added in her 'totally disinterested' voice.

Well, I've been at this MAGIC game long enough not to be distracted. Bossy Bossom is quite frail in the head department, so I figured two verses should be enough for her.

'**SPIRo, SPERo, SQUIGGLEoUS SCoTCH,**
CAST YoUR EYES WHITHER MY WATCH.'

I said twice.

Miss Bossom watched my **MAGIC POCKET WATCH** on its chain going backwards and forwards, forwards and backwards in front of her nose like a lizard watching one of those massive flies that skulk around Grandpa's larder.

'Miss Bossom, you will change my casting. I don't want to be a duck. Some people might think of me as a perfect Cinderella . . . not that I'm saying it has to be her.'

'YES, HOLLY, OF COURSE.'

But before I could issue any other 'indications', guess who came creeping back into the classroom. Felicity Snoop, not minding her own business. So I had to put my **MAGIC POCKET WATCH** back into my pocket pretty PROMPTO.

Anyway, the job was done, *I thought*.

229

But when I got home **BIGGER NEWS** had overtaken the newsworthiness of my scandalous treatment. **THREE THINGS**, in fact:

1 Mrs Smartside has invited Mum and Dad to go round to her house to play bridge.* Dad pointed out that they don't know how to play bridge, **nor** any of the rules.

2 Mum's company has taken over the PR for something called *School of Rock*.

'Is that Geology?' I asked.

'No, Holly . . . deary me . . . it's a **big** hit musical in the West End by Lord Andrew Lloyd Webber . . . Don't they teach you **anything** at school?'

'Excuse you . . . **don't** talk to me about my school,' I replied in my 'OUTRAGED' voice. 'My teacher lives in a parallel universe** . . . she thinks there are ducks in *Cinderella*.'

---

* BRIDGE – card game adults play where they build a bridge out of cards.

** PARALLEL UNIVERSE – floats around in space doing geometry.

Mum wasn't listening – her new job starts with immediate effect. She is going to watch the show in two days' time, lucky thing. But I am very proud of her.

Harold and Stickly were holding their first official band practice – and they made a terrific noise. Stickly can make some really goofy TWANGING noises with his guitar and he has some good stretching moves – a bit like Mum does in Pilates. And Harold can hit his drums pretty hard and in double-whopper quick time.

Harmony arrived with her notebook and sat around looking CREATIVE, which added to the scene.

When they stick to other people's famous songs they are *top notch* – but when they start all that 'this is one of our new songs' lark they are GARBAGE. (And all of Harold and Stickly's songs are new, of course – brand new – the paint's still wet.)

I fear that my birthday song royalties are going to be very **thin** pickings!

Then I remembered the band poster I saw at the Chequers. →

So I told them,

'CUT OUT THE NEW RUBBISH AND I'LL GET YOU A GIG.'

They're pretty excited that Holly Hopkinson (BAND MANAGER INC) is putting her neck on the line for them. Before bed I said to Grandpa, 'Why don't you see if you can get Harold and Stickly a gig at the Chequers?'

PS In spite of exciting times ahead for Holly Hopkinson (BAND MANAGER INC), Holly Hopkinson [VILLAGE SCHOOL-GOER) is

OFFICIALLY NOT HAPPY –

I do not look, sound or feel like **a duck**.

WHEN MY MEMOIRS ARE PUBLISHED BOSSY BOSSOM IS GOING TO SERIOUSLY REGRET THIS DAY UNLESS SHE SPIT-SPOT UPGRADES MY PART.

CHAPTER 36

A VERY DARK HOUR

~~~~~~

DAFFODIL CALLED AN OFFICIAL
EMERGENCY TOP-FLIGHT SUMMIT
MEETING THE NEXT MORNING ON THE
SCHOOL BUS, WELL OUT OF EARSHOT
OF SLINKY DAVE.

'**W**e need to ACT . . . I am *not* spending the next few weeks laying eggs,' she declared.

Daffodil is much **tougher** than she looks. *But* there was no way, José, that I could tell her that I already *had* acted – only 'just for me', as they say in Switzerland. Of course, if I'd had more time, I *would* have sorted Daffodil's part out too.

A trail of **SCORCHED** earth followed my feet from Slinky Dave's bus to the noticeboard. I was going to play it super cool when the news broke that I'd been drafted in overnight to scoop up one of the big parts. No swanking – just a cool raised eyebrow.

But who was standing by the board with the final cast pinned up on it, sniggering from foot to foot? Felicity Snoop, of course.

'I see you've landed a new part,' she said.

And I had – there it was in **BLACK** and WHITE.

HOLLY HOPKINSON - SECOND CHICKEN, *ELDORADO*.

My **MAGIC POCKET WATCH** has let me down badly.

Maybe the **MAGIC** has *run out*?

THIS IS A VERY **DARK HOUR** FOR HOLLY HOPKINSON.

Felicity Snoop spent all day loving every second of me walking around clucking and laying (wooden) eggs all over the place while she sang like a demented, out-of-tune cat to Prince **UN**=charming.

~ *VINNIE NEWS* ~

By the way, *he* still hasn't shown his face at the farm since the beginning of school, and is acting like he can't see me at school. He is officially **BLACKLISTED**.

So all in all it was the worst day I have **EVER HAD** at school. I chucked the **PoCKET WATCH** under my bed when I got home. It can gather some dust there as far as I'm concerned – useless thing. And I shall be having words with Aunt Electra about her so-called **MAGIC** present.

CHAPTER 37

THE REST IS DOWN TO YOU

THE **BIG NEWS** WHEN I GOT HOME FROM SCHOOL WAS THAT EVENTS WERE MOVING FAST FOR HAROLD AND STICKLY. GRANDPA HAS CREATED A RECORDING STUDIO FOR THEM BY MOVING SOME OLD MACHINERY OUT OF ONE OF HIS BARNS. IT'S A BIT WHIFFY IN THERE, BUT THAT'S ROCK AND ROLL, BABY.

But as I am now officially worried about Grandpa's finances, I suggested that he should take a percentage of all their future earnings if he's laying on an old cowshed for them; and told him that I can draw up contracts if he signs on the DOTTED LINE.

Of course, I shall be taking an appropriate* cut seeing as I am already the manager.

* APPROPRIATE – massive rip-off.

Grandpa said he just wants to be able to watch the racing in peace. I don't think he takes money very seriously.

Anyway, that isn't all. Grandpa had a word with the people at the Chequers at lunchtime and the result is that I am in a position to announce some

TOUR NEWS!

Harold and His Band

are doing a twilight evening gig.

(THAT'S THEIR **UNOFFICIAL** NAME UNTIL THEY THINK OF AN **OFFICIAL NAME.**)

LATE BREAKING
MAGIC POCKET WATCH *NEWS* –
Aunt Electra was hanging around after supper, so I officially summoned her into the Bedouin tent for 'a little chat'.

'*It's stopped working*,' I told her.

'What do you mean?' she asked.

'My **MAGIC** watch has stopped working. I hypnotised Miss Bossom, and she said she'd change me from being a duck into Cinderella, or something big, and she changed me into the *second* chicken.'

'Oh dear,' said Aunt Electra with a stupid smile on her face. 'It hasn't stopped working, Holly, but you *have* forgotten how to work it.'

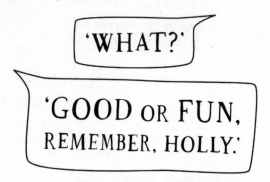

'WHAT?'

'GOOD OR FUN, REMEMBER, HOLLY.'

I frowned. 'But that doesn't make sense . . . it was going to be good for me not being a duck . . . and it is not good for me being a chicken, thank you very much!'

'You are going to have to learn to work with the watch, not just use it as a servant . . . that's all I can say at this stage . . . the rest is down to you.' And with that she gave me a MARSHMALLOW KISS and flounced off like aunts from Bohemia do.

I HAVE NO IDEA WHAT SHE IS TALKING ABOUT. THIS IS A DISASTER.

CHAPTER 38

GETTING BACK IN THE SADDLE

THIS MORNING I WAS THINKING ABOUT WHAT AUNT ELECTRA HAD SAID ABOUT THE WATCH NOT BEING BROKEN, BUT ME BEING A SHAMBLES AND FORGETTING HOW TO USE IT. RELUCTANTLY, I FISHED IT OUT FROM UNDER MY BED AND TURNED IT OVER IN MY HAND. AFTER ALL, IF I WASN'T GOING TO BE A CHICKEN IN THE SCHOOL SHOW, I NEEDED TO DO SOMETHING.

I HAD TO MAKE THE WATCH WORK AGAIN.

But first, I needed a guinea pig.

Or a horse.

Beanstalk was lounging around with High Five in the mud as usual in their field, so I decided it was time to 'get back in the saddle' as they say in the films.

I leaned over the fence and concentrated really hard, waving my heavy **MAGIC POCKET WATCH** in front of Beanstalk's nose, nice and slowly. Maybe that was what I got **wrong** with Miss Bossom? Maybe I was **too quick**?

> ## *MUSCLE NEWS* –
> my **MAGIC POCKET WATCH** is quite heavy, so I am developing **very** big muscles in my right arm.

'**SPIRO, SPERO, SQUIGGLEOUS SCOTCH CAST YOUR EYES WHITHER MY WATCH.**'

I said three times.

'Beanstalk, stand up on your hind legs,' I commanded.

Beanstalk gave a bit of a yawn and eyed the watch with deep IRRITATION – but she did get up, out of the mud, and stand on two legs, with her front hooves up in the air!

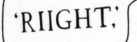
'RIIGHT,'

said Vince in farmer speak, wandering over.

I put away the watch hurriedly.

'ER, HOW DO YOU DO?'

I said in a PANIC. And even Vince knew that was a weird thing to say to someone you already know.

'Riight . . . never seen 'un do that,' said Vince, inspired to actual speech by the sight of Beanstalk on two legs.

So Aunt Electra was right – my **MAGIC POCKET WATCH** hasn't lost its power – but I still don't know why.

SO NOW I AM EVEN MORE CONFUSED.

On the positive side, there was some **GOOD PARENT NEWS** – when I was off to bed this evening, guess who was in the sitting room huddled up like besties. Mum and Aunt Electra. So the Big Fat Cake-off truce is holding.

I **EARWIGGED** their conversation for a bit from behind the sofa – and Aunt Electra is going to help out at the farm now and again when her schedule permits as Dad is getting a bit busier on the cooking front. Which is good news all round.

It even made me forget about being Second Chicken for a moment.

PS On that matter, I am NOT going to be Second Chicken and lay pretend eggs while Felicity Snoop laughs at me for the rest of my life.

YOU SHOULD NOT HAVE TO GO AROUND LAYING EGGS IF YOU HAVE A **MAGIC POCKET WATCH**.

NO WAY, JOSÉ.

CHAPTER 39

THE GIG IS UP

IF ANYONE EVER TELLS YOU IT'S EASY
BEING A BAND MANAGER, THEN THEY ARE
PROBABLY NOT A BAND MANAGER.

So we arrived at the Chequers and everything was great. They'd cleared an area in the corner where there was an electric plug that Stickly needs, and there were a few bowls of crisps and nuts on a little table to keep my boys going.

'WANT SOME NUTS, HAROLD?' I asked.

'Whateva,' was the sum of his reply. Pop stars get like that when they're doing a gig. Although Harold is *always* like that.

'Ooh, look,' I added. 'Practically the whole village is here.' It was true: our entire extended family had turned up, including Barkley and Beanstalk, but also a load of farmers who I hadn't seen before.

Well, I say a load. Really it was about twenty people, total. And Dad's cricketing butcher friend, Sir Garfield, had come to make sure the FREE drinks didn't get warm, by the looks of things.

FREE
DRINKS

Aunt Electra was standing at the front and sort of sway-dancing, even though there wasn't any music yet.

'I'M GOING TO BE SICK,'

Harold said as he made a runner for the BOGS.

He looked dead WHITE when he came back – but I told him the show had to go on. So Stickly started twanging away but all Harold did was sit there looking at his sticks.

'Start hitting something, you moose,' I hissed. 'Or I'll come and hit *you*.'

Harold started aiming at his drums, but he was all over the place. It sounded **TERRIBLE**, even to an untrained ear like mine. Even Barkley and Beanstalk looked pretty horrified.

After two songs I grabbed Harold's mike, which he hadn't even made a sound into, and told the crowd that,

'THE BOYS ARE JUST GOING TO TAKE A QUICK BREAK.'

We stepped away from the stage.

'Harold . . . excuse you, but what the flipping heck are you playing at?' I asked in my 'BAND MANAGER' voice.

'I DON'T KNOW . . . I CAN'T THINK . . . WHATEVA . . . MY BRAIN'S FROZEN . . . MY HANDS TOO . . .'

'You are kidding me.'

'I've never played in front of this many people before,' he whimpered.

'What are you talking about, Harold? Slinky Dave gets more people in his bus than there are in this bar.'

'Whateva . . . I can't go on . . . I'm going home,' Harold sniffled, and that was that, off he hopped. Like a lamentable, lame LEVERET.

Then guess who was all over Stickly like a cheap suit on National Cheap Suit Day – my sister Harmony – and if I didn't know better, I would say she was looking a bit **BOGGLE-EYED!** I wonder if she caught something off Bossy Bossom at the fete?

CALL THE RIOT POLICE – IT'S ALL GOING OFF IN LOWER GORING.

o o o

I walked home with Mum, Dad, Aunt Electra and Grandpa, and Barkley and Beanstalk.

Mum said, 'Poor lamb. I had no idea he'd get stage fright so badly . . . and it's been lovely to see him come out of his shell a bit and actually do something.'

Dad just rolled his eyes and said 'Events, dear boy, events,' in his 'stupid' voice.

I just ignored their ridiculous adult chat all the way home and hatched a plan for me and my **MAGIC POCKET WATCH** to rescue the musical *and financial* fortunes of the Hopkinson family from the sewers of **DESPAIR**.

PS If word gets out about this RUBBISH gig my credo-biography will be shot to pieces, so I'm having a total official media BLACKOUT on the whole evening.

I suppose when I win one of those 'Service to the Music Industry' awards where you get up on stage and talk about yourself, I might let slip about tonight. And everyone will laugh like they can't really believe that happened.

CHAPTER 40

FASTEN YOUR SEATBELTS

DAFFODIL WAS STILL IN A DARK PLACE WHEN I GOT ON THE SCHOOL BUS THIS MORNING. BEING A DOMESTICATED FOWL RATHER THAN SOMETHING MORE EXOTIC IN THE CHRISTMAS SHOW HAS DAMAGED HER MOJO.

'I have a plan,' I said to Daffodil in my 'confident' voice. 'I will save you. Miss Bossom will be having a trip to London shortly, whether she likes it or not, that might just undermine her confidence in her goofy play and flush it down the BOG.'

Daffodil looked dubious, but I told her, 'Courage, *mon fils*,' as they say in Botswana.

But courage on the school bus and courage under fire are two very distant cousins who haven't met since their parents fell out at a wedding.

What was I thinking, I thought as I approached Miss Bossom's desk with my **MAGIC POCKET WATCH** weighing heavy in my hand. Last time I tried it on her, all that happened was she changed me from a waterfowl to a farmyard fowl.

THIS COULD BE THE MOST HUMILIATING MOMENT OF MY LIFE.

'Can I have a word, please, miss?' I said.

'Certainly . . . What's troubling you, Holly?' she asked.

'Nothing much, but can you just look at my **MAGIC POCKET WATCH**, please?'

'Oh, isn't it nice,' she said.

I gave her three verses of **SPIRO, SPERO** – the same as High Five.

'Miss Bossom, you are going to take our class to London to watch *School of Rock* . . . my mum can fix us up with tickets, and Slinky Dave can drive us.' I was sure if she saw how good a *real* musical was, she'd realise how rubbish her Cinders show was, and spit-spot do something about it.

'Yes, Holly,' she said obediently.

'You will?'

'Yes, Holly.'

ZIP-A-DEE-DOO-DAH.

It looked like my **MAGIC POCKET WATCH** and I were back on track – cooking on gas!

'And you will buy us as much popcorn as we want in the interval?' I added, just to make sure.

'YES, HOLLY.'

255

'Good, well, that's settled, then,' I said in my 'phew' voice. 'Come along, Miss Bossom, we'll be late for lunch. Spit-spot.'

THANK GOODNESS I've got my MOJO back.

Thank you, world.

Here comes Holly – fasten your SEATBELTS.

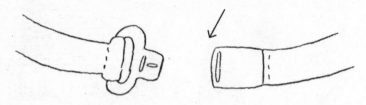

Mum arrived home full of chat about *School of Rock*. But something told me it might not be all plain sailing getting her under the spell of my MAGIC POCKET WATCH.

You know how some adults can be tricky if they're not concentrating? Well, Mum is one of them. So I snuck up behind her while she had her head in the deep freeze, and wiggled my MAGIC POCKET WATCH in front of her nose four times once she'd retrieved the frozen Brussels sprouts she was hunting for. Which is quite a big dose.

'Mum, you *are* going to take my whole class and Miss Bossom to a performance of *School of Rock* this weekend. You can tell Andrew Lord that you must have your own focus group check the gig out.'

'Of course, Holly,' Mum said in her 'surprised PR' voice. 'What a good idea.'

Then, in the spirit of the Hopkinson family pulling together, I added, 'And I think we should take Harold and Stickly with us . . . now they've formed a band and are officially in the music business with me . . . Harold needs a bit of perspiration.'*

'YES, HOLLY . . . WHATEVER YOU SAY.'

* PERSPIRATION – sweating while you have good ideas.

And then in a double-whopper fit of niceness I also said, 'And a little bird tells me that Harmony might want to come if Stickly is.'

'YES, HOLLY.'

BINGO DE PINGO.

Aunts formally known as Ethel are great – but *mums* are irreplaceable.

CHAPTER 41

A VERY EMOTIONAL DAY

CELEBRITY NEWS - WE'RE OFF TO LONDON TOWN TODAY TO SEE *SCHOOL OF ROCK*. WITH A MASSIVE - ADMITTEDLY RATHER BIZARRE - PICNIC FROM DAD. BEANSTALK TRIED TO GET ON THE BUS, BUT MUM JUST SAID, 'NO WAY.'

THIS TOPS GOING TO SEE THE QUEEN. It is a very emotional day and I have the teeniest tiniest wavering bit of hope that Aleeshaa might be there to share it with me. I got Mum to text her mum *again*, so who knows . . .

Anyway, Dad is really **expanding** his cooking repertoire, and doing commissions for the posh ladies in the village has made him go *stratospheric* with his food choices.

PICNIC ☆ WE HAVE

☆ avocado and lemon mousse
← (NICE BUT QUITE WOBBLY).

☆ cold chicken-and-turkey terrine
← (A BIT WARM).

☆ homemade Scotch eggs
← (NOT SURE ABOUT PUTTING THE MEAT ROUND THE EGGS).

☆ gooseberry fool
← (DEE-LICIOUS, EVEN IF DAFFODIL SAYS IT LOOKS LIKE IT'S COME FROM VINNIE'S NOSE)

☆ and some cheese that Dad has made from Florence's milk
← (DISASTER – NEVER MIND).

I'd have preferred a cheese sandwich and some crisps, if I'm honest.

Slinky Dave had the bus ready to go at eleven sharp, smelling like he does these days – all perfume-y and GROSS.

SEATING NEWS – When Vinnie got on the bus, instead of going to sit with Wolfe, Gaspar and Tiger near the back row, he came and sat next to me, Daffodil and Brian.

'All riight,' he said as if nothing had ever happened. 'Can I sit 'ere?'

Of course I was about to tell him to sling his hook, but all the other boys, led by Gaspar, were making HISSING noises at him, and I figured out what he was doing. He was *finally* standing up to them and showing them he wasn't afraid to be my mate.

So I said, 'Yorkel,' and told him that I would be delighted if he'd sit with me and Daffodil. So he did, and his mates laughed at him, but he just ignored them, which gave me a warm feeling inside. Like curry does.

Miss Bossom and Mum had a bit of a head-to-head on who knew the most about *School of Rock* and Andrew Lord.

Miss Bossom boasted that she once got down to the shortlist for one of his parts and all the boys laughed – they thought she was telling PORKIES.

Harold, Stickly and Harmony sat right at the back of the coach. I think they're beyond grateful to be back in a land where they don't have to stand on tiptoes to get a phone signal.

Harmony was winding herself up at breakfast, saying, '*School of Rock* is sooo, like, abuse of children and child labour. They should basically be, like, at school, not working.'

'Ha ha . . . very funny, Harmony,' Dad said. 'They should be at school . . . like, get it? Anyway, it's hardly a New York SWEATSHOP.'

'WELL... I'VE, LIKE, SOOO GOT SOME **FRIENDS** COMING TO **PROTEST** OUTSIDE THE THEATRE,'

Harmony said.

'Friends . . . what friends?' I asked as flipping alarm bells began to make a double-whopper racket in my head.

'Like . . . my online friends.'

When Slinky Dave pulled the bus up outside the theatre, there was a RABBLE of human creatures on the pavement revolting. Most of them had **BLACK** balaclavas on.

Harmony went a bit white around the gills and gulped.

'Your friends?' I enquired.

'Like . . . I don't think so,' she said.

But unfortunately for her, they unravelled one of their banners.

263

'HOPKINSONS ECO-WARRIORS AGAINST CHILD LABOUR' it read.

Then they started chucking stuff at Slinky Dave's bus; what a panic monkey he is. Miss Bossom practically had to wrench the steering wheel out of his hands!

Then Mum started to have a HAIRY FIT with Harmony.

'Harmony, who are those people?'

'Basically they're, like, from the char-it-tee, I think,' Harmony spluttered as a cloud of amnesia settled over her.

'They're, like . . . sooo nothing to do with me.'

'What about their Hopkinson banner?' I asked loudly.

Harmony gave me one of her looks.

I think 'the Hopkinson family pulling together' mode is officially over with her.

'Harmony . . . make them protest somewhere else . . . *now*,' Mum said in her 'this-is-your-final-warning' voice.

'Like, where?'

'I DON'T CARE! YOU CAN SEND THEM TO THE MOON, IF YOU LIKE. JUST GET THEM AWAY FROM HERE!'

While everyone was distracted I grabbed the MOMENTO, as they say in Bratislava, and waved my MAGIC POCKET WATCH in front of Harold's nose three times.

'SPIRO, SPERO, SQUIGGLEOUS SCOTCH,
CAST YOUR EYES WHITHER MY WATCH.'

'Right, Harold,' I said urgently. 'You will sign this contract now . . . it's for your own good . . . otherwise one of those music lapels* will nick all your money.'

'WHATEVA, HOLLY.'

Then I added, 'Harold, at half time we're going backstage and *you* are going to take over from the kid who is the drummer . . . he will need a rest.'

So, after his debacle in the Chequers, you might be thinking that I am a total *nutter* trying to turn a sow's purse into a silk ear! But I know Harold can do it if he doesn't know he's doing it – if you get my drift.

'WHATEVA.'

And then I added the important bit. 'Harold, I know what your problem is . . . why you're always so STROPPY . . . underneath it all, you're actually very shy . . . and you don't want anyone to know that . . . well, from now on you are never going to be shy again.'

266

* MUSIC LAPEL – man in swanky suit who runs a music label.

And now I really was wondering if I was pushing my luck with the **MAGIC POCKET WATCH**.

'Thank you, Holly, I will never be shy again,' he said in a rather 'sweet' voice I'd never heard before. And he looked quite pleased. So I felt like I'd done something really *good*.

'Right, let's get inside before Harmony's friends get us all arrested,' I suggested to Botty Bossom.

'Do not admit to knowing your sister to *anyone*,' Mum hissed at me.

'Not even Andrew Lord?'

'Who . . . yes . . . particularly him . . . why on Earth did we bring her?'

Well, obviously I couldn't tell Mum about *that*! Not yet, anyway.

THE WORLD OF **MAGIC** IS NOT ALL ROSES AND SPARKLERS – it's not as easy as you may think, I can tell you.

I was a double-whopper nervous flipping WRECK walking into the theatre.

CHAPTER 42

HOLLY HOPKINSON'S SCHOOL OF ROCK

THE THEATRE **WASN'T** WHAT THE OTHER KIDS WERE EXPECTING. THAT'S A CHIPPING TOPLEY UPBRINGING FOR YOU.

'I thought theatres were all dead posh with chandeliers and wallpaper on the ceiling,' piped up Crocus.

'They need to get some decorators in,' added Amaryllis.

'Your mum would love to get her hands on this,' smirked Felicity Snoop to Daffodil. 'Can you imagine – scented candles and floral cushions all over the place.'

Daffodil looked like she was going to SOCK her one.

'It's urban clique,'* I told Felicity. 'It's EDGY and COOL. And guess what . . . there's nowhere for you to tie your pony up.' Thank you very much.

Mum told us in her 'go-to-bed' voice that we had to be low key and not make any noise, in case we disturbed Andrew Lord. So it was indoor voices all round.

'I love popcorn,' said Daffodil when she'd got over the business with Felicity.

'No way Miss Bossom will let us have any of that . . . it makes your teeth fall out,' said Iris.

So I was looking like the bee's knees when I asked Miss Bossom for large popcorns all round and she said yes.

HOLLY HOPKINSON IS IN THE HOUSE.

Our seats were right at the back, but we were near the people who twiddled with the buttons to do the lights up and down and stuff.

* CLIQUE – fashion look that close group of friends all like.

So this is the story – the teacher and the kids in the play are being NAUGHTY and spending all of their lessons being a band, encouraged by their 'bad' substitute teacher. So they are not doing any other schoolwork.

The parents and the other teachers will *not* be happy when they find out. But the kids all love playing instruments and the band are going to win a big competition.

I have never heard such a flipping RACKET in all my life – but Daffodil was loving it.

By half time, I felt like my head had been inside a washing machine on the synthetics cycle. But Holly Hopkinson (BAND MANAGER INC) had work to do.

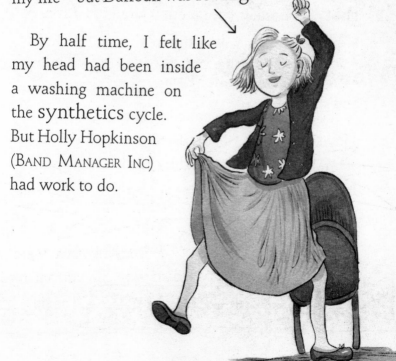

So, while Miss Bossom took all the other kids for more popcorn and an inside WEE, I reminded Mum I wanted to meet Andrew Lord – who was playing with knobs on the lighting desk near us anyway. I needed a chat with him for my Harold plan.

My knees were knocking together like cymbals – I could hardly see myself think. It was one thing to 'cook' a couple of members of your own family and a doofus like Miss Bossom – but a global phenomenon was a different fish course altogether.

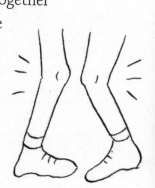

'Er . . .' Mum was babbling nervously, '. . . Lord Lloyd Webber . . .' (SHE GETS IN A MUDDLE WITH NAMES) 'this is my daughter Holly,' Mum said in her 'Mrs Smartside' voice.

'OH . . . HELLO,' he replied, looking up from his knobs.

'HOW DO YOU DO, MR LORD,' I said.

Fortunately Mum got distracted with some focus grouping, so I grabbed Lord's lapels by their horns and dived in.

'Great show . . . do you like my **MAGIC POCKET WATCH**?' I asked, waving it in front of his nose. I only gave him two verses because he spends a lot of time in the **DARK** so he must have very good eyesight.

'Well, funnily enough, I have a rather good collection of those,' he said, watching it like a hawk.

'Is that a Waltham and Elgin, by any chance?'

'No, it's a bit later than that,' I said, winging it. And somewhat put out that I was dealing with a watch expert just when I wasn't expecting it.

'But, Mr Lord . . . *you* want my brother, Harold, to take over on the drums at half time,' I suggested.

In fact, I was getting ready to run for it, if I'm honest, because Andrew Lord looked like he could properly kick off if you meddled with his team selection.

But double-whopper phew – he said, 'Yes, of course . . . that's actually rather a *good* idea. The other fellow is just a bit off tonight.'

'Yes, that's what I thought,' I lied, trying to regain control of my knees.

In the music-management business you've got to sound like you know what you're talking about. But no one's got a clue, really. What is poetry to one man is a noise abatement court judgement* to another.

So Andrew Lord took me and Harold backstage and we got Harold togged out for the second half. Harold had to sign something called a disclaimer – which set my alarm bells flashing; we could have been signing away his life's work.

When they all came back on for the second half, I was shaking like a leaf. If Harold makes a complete **DOOFUS** of himself, I am for the high jump. You can just read the headlines now:

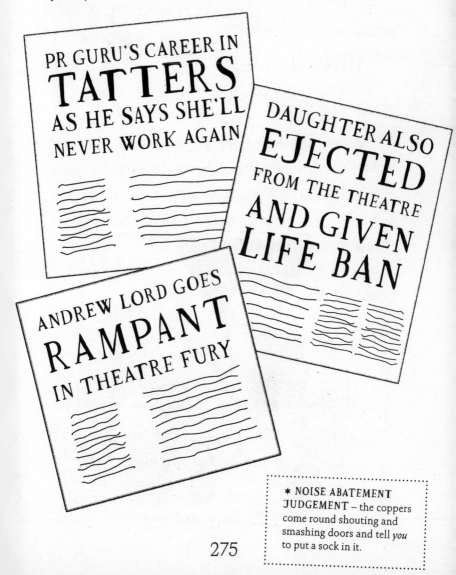

PR GURU'S CAREER IN
TATTERS
AS HE SAYS SHE'LL
NEVER WORK AGAIN

DAUGHTER ALSO
EJECTED
FROM THE THEATRE
AND GIVEN
LIFE BAN

ANDREW LORD GOES
RAMPANT
IN THEATRE FURY

* NOISE ABATEMENT
JUDGEMENT – the coppers
come round shouting and
smashing doors and tell *you*
to put a sock in it.

But, as it happened, Harold knocked it out of the park.

DOUBLE-WHOPPER BINGO À LA ZINGO-STYLE.

He was like a **raging bull,** tossing his head about like his lice were driving him **MAD.** And hitting his cymbals in treble time and all that sort of stuff.

Stickly could *not* believe his eyes ànd, boy, did I rub it into Felicity Snoop that *my* brother was on the drums.

This is a **big moment** in the life of Holly Hopkinson:

1. This is the first time I've got one over Felicity 'Slippery' Snoop.
   THANK YOU VERY MUCH.

2. Even though he can be a massive doofus, I'm glad that I've helped Harold out; and got him over his stage-fright thing.

3. My MAGIC POCKET WATCH is working again on double-whopper full steam ahead.
   TRIUMPHO (AS THEY SAY IN ROME).

CHAPTER 43

MY EUREKA MOMENT

THEN GUESS WHAT HAPPENED – *CELEBRITY NEWS!*

I saw this ginger mop bouncing towards me. And Daffodil squealed, 'Holly . . . it's the most famous singer in the world . . . right here.'

'WHAT . . . HIM . . . THE ONE WITH GINGER HAIR ALL OVER THE PLACE?' I asked.

'Yeees . . . you MUST know who he is . . . it's Ed Sheeran . . . he's sold over a hundred million records.'

Well, you can't be a big shot in the music business like me and not know who Ed Shear'um is without looking like a right doofus, so I had to wing it a bit.

'Of course I know who *he* is,' I said quickly. And then he flipping well walked right up to me.

'Hi there,' he said in a dead-cool voice. 'I'm Ed . . . nice to meet you.'

'I'm Holly,' I gulped. 'And this is my associate, Daffodil. But Daffodil was not playing it cool, so I motioned to her to vamoose with a few flicks of my hand.

'Wow . . . wasn't that drummer great?' he said, his eyes suddenly looking as wild as his hair.

'Not bad.' I nodded. 'He's one of mine actually . . . would you like to come backstage and meet him?'

'Well, I'm in a bit of a rush right now,' Ed said. 'I'm off to a gig.'

So, quick as a flash – which is what you've got to be in this business – I got my **MAGIC POCKET WATCH** out and swivelled it in front of his nose.

You see, I had an idea about the school play, which I have to admit was inspired by Mum trying to rope in celebrities to open the village fete.

'**SPIRO, SPERO, SQUIGGLEOUS SCOTCH, CAST YOUR EYES WHITHER MY WATCH!**'

I commanded.

279

And I gave him four verses to be safe as he was bobbing all over the place.

'We're doing a school Christmas show and we need to raise lots of funds to save the school roof . . . Will you come . . . you can help us sell tickets?'

'IS IT GOING TO BE ONE OF THOSE **BORING ONES?**'

Ed asked, pulling a face.

And then I had my Eureka moment on the Road to Damascus.*

'No . . . not at all . . . in fact, we're going to do *School of Rock*,' I said. 'It will be flipping noisy, but I can't help that . . . that's the way they roll.'

Of course I was winging it a bit, but if you're in PR you always hold some of the facts back.

'Well, I'll definitely come if you're going to do that . . . Where's your school?'

'Er . . . it's in Lower Goring . . . near Chipping Topley.'

> * EUREKA MOMENT ON THE ROAD TO DAMASCUS – when you're walking along and then you start running around like a lunatic shouting because you're so happy.

'Shape of you,' he said, going up for a high five.

'Excuse you and pardon your French,' I replied. Just because he's a mega does not mean he can get cheeky with Holly Hopkinson, worldwide chief executive of 'Drummers Are Us' corporation (soon to be launched). You have to watch these pop-star types.

On the bus I told Daffodil confidentially that Ed was coming to the school show and that *I* had arranged it.

'OH EM GEE!' she said. 'You're the best.'

So that's that, Felicity Snoop! Holly Hopkinson:

FIRING on all cylinders.

And even I didn't think the day could get any bigger until we got home.

RACING NEWS – Grandpa was tearing around in the kitchen like a spaniel trying to eat its tail – the queen's horse Fist Bump is running at Cheltenham tomorrow.

ONE LAST PIECE OF NEWS – Aunt Electra was all ears when we got back to the farm.

> 'DID EVERYONE HAVE A NICE DAY ...
> DID YOU DO LOTS OF GOOD
> THINGS ... WAS IT FUN?'

she asked once we were sure there were no prying eyes listening to us.

'Yes, yes ... it's working again,' I reported.

'And have we worked out why?' Aunt Electra asked, doing stupid things with her eyebrows that only adults do.

'Well, I think the speed I say the **SPIRO, SPERO** verse is important ... not too quick.'

> 'YE-ES.'

'And the dose has got to be right ... defo not too little ... too much "OVERCOOK" is a bit dodge too.'

'YE-ES . . . ANYTHING **ELSE?**'

'Oh, I don't know, Aunt Electra.'

'Well, did Harold have a *fun* day?'

'Great fun.'

'And was it *good* to see him playing on stage, and not getting stage fright?'

'Yes, really good. It gave me a curry feeling inside.'

'So there you are . . . you have your answer.'

Don't ask me what she was talking about. Why do adults always talk in RIDDLES and make it up as they go along!

PS Aleeshaa didn't show up. She is *officially* not even my best London friend any more, and history will reflect on her being a fickle turncoat.

CHAPTER 44

THE LOOK OF EAGLES

I *DID* **NOT** SLEEP LAST NIGHT.
BY TOMORROW NIGHT HIGH FIVE COULD
BE WORTH A **FORTUNE** IF HIS BROTHER
FIST BUMP **WINS** FOR THE QUEEN AT
CHELTENHAM ... OR NOTHING,
IF HE **DOESN'T.**

Mum had to get the early train to London 'to see if I've still got a job'. Although I think she's getting her undies in a twist over nothing because Andrew Lord was very pleased with Harold's drumming.

I'm not sure how much my **MAGIC POCKET WATCH** can help out with a horse race – but it has at least helped me out with getting Dad to excuse me from school today.

CACHINGO

As soon as Mum was out of earshot Dad got on the phone to Ms Growler.

'I'm very sorry,' he said, 'but Holly is running a significant temperature this morning, and I think it would be rather *irresponsible* to bring her to school today.' Nice one, Dad. Even nicer one, MAGIC POCKET WATCH.

While Grandpa and I went through the runners in the *Racing Post*, Dad made all of us Gor May* sandwiches – although they were actually roast beef with horseradish (no horse) and coronation chicken, which seemed appropriate as we were off to support the queen's horse.

(Did you know that when the queen got crowned everyone was partying so hard some idiot spilled curry powder into the mayonnaise and then poured it over the cold chicken? But they were so hungry they ate it anyway.)

285

* GOR MAY – A woman called May, who was such a good cook everyone said 'Gor-blimey' when they ate her food.

As a special treat, we went on the race train – which is very different from Mum's computer train. Beanstalk was dead keen on coming, but we decided that she might get us *unwanted* attention and blow my cover. And guess who happened to be on the train heading in the same direction as us?

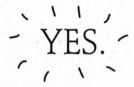

YES.

Dad's butcher, cricketing friend Sir Garfield.

> 'SIR GARFIELD . . . WHAT ARE YOU **ACTUALLY** DOING HEADING IN THE **SAME** DIRECTION AS US ON THIS TRAIN?'

'Going racing, of course . . . . I love racing as much as I love cricket . . . my dad used to take me every Sunday in Barbados when I was your age.'

'Oh,' I replied.

Dad said, 'This beats driving,' as we had a drink and ate our coronation-chicken sandwiches. I told Dad he should try chucking some curry powder into some random things to see what he could create. Ice cream, maybe? Or stew? You never know until you try.

Grandpa said, 'This horse can definitely win today,' quite a few times. I think what he meant was, 'I need this horse to win today.'

When we got to the racecourse, the horses were walking around 'the paddock' for the first race. They looked strong and FAST.

The jockeys looked like they didn't get much to eat – they were very short and thin and pale. But the blokes who Grandpa says are the trainers looked like they'd made up for the jockeys. They all had big, red faces and even **bigger** bellies.

The crowd **roared** its head off when the horses came past in the first race.

'This is much better than going to school with a temperature,' I told Grandpa in my '**SICK**' voice.

Then the next race was Fist Bump's.

There were eight runners in the race – and Fist Bump was number eight.

'That's his trainer,' said Sir Garfield as some bloke who was 'poured into his clothes and forgot to say when' walked past with a funny brown hat on.

So I followed him – Sir Garfield and Dad were too busy looking at the other horses to notice I'd gone – and slipped into Fist Bump's stable.

I got my **MAGIC POCKET WATCH** out of my secret belt and waved it in front of his nose eight times – I wasn't taking any chances with this one.

'YOU ARE GOING TO **WIN**,' I told Fist Bump.

He nodded and then the door of the stable opened and guess who walked in?

Only the queen and the man wearing the funny hat.

'One thinks he looks very well, Lord Dorchester,' she said to the man with her.

'Yes,' he said, rubbing his hands and narrowing his eyes. 'Today is the day.'

And then he saw me in the corner.

'OI . . . WHAT ARE YOU DOING IN HERE . . . HOP IT,' he shouted.

'Oh . . . it's the young lady from the Royal Society of Young Gardeners,' said the queen.

'Hello, ma'am,' I said, doing a massive curtsy like Daffodil's. 'Er . . . I'm just checking the MANURE situation . . . thought this might be a good place to find some for the roses.'

'Yes, one thinks that's a rather good idea,' agreed the queen. 'How's your little friend? Daffodil, isn't it?'

'Oh, very well, thank you,' I replied, being cool.

'STILL DRINKING TEA, IS SHE?'

'Oh, yes . . . she loves her cuppa.'

'Such a sensible drink in the afternoon.'

'Well, I must be off . . . lots of pruning to do, you know,' I said, thinking fast on my feet.

Dad, Grandpa and Sir Garfield were looking tense when I got back, so I told them the queen was very pleased with Fist Bump. They looked at me like I'm a double-whopper DOOFUS.

The queen's racing colours are beautiful – Mrs Chichester should copy them for her cushions; a purple and scarlet jacket with gold braiding, and a black cap.

The jockey looked super cool as he cantered out on to the course – Fist Bump had 'the look of eagles', Grandpa said. (Which I think is a good thing.)

When the race started, Fist Bump was nearly last.

Oh no, I thought. *I'm going to spend the rest of my life biking up hills on an old bicycle delivering pizzas.*

Then Fist Bump started to make a move.

Dad started shouting like a lunatic.

I couldn't see a flipping thing – but the commentator roared, 'They're coming to the last and its anyone's race.'

Then he added, 'As they flash past the post, Fist Bump has got up. Fist Bump is the winner.'

Sir Garfield started JIGGING around like he had a load of ferrets down his trousers and started hugging Grandpa, and Dad picked me up and squeezed the **PIPS** out of me, thank you very much.

Then Dad was tossing me up in the air and catching me, and **whooping**, and I have to admit, I **whooped** a bit too.

Then I looked around a bit nervously. I was suddenly worried there might be TV cameras at the races, and quite a lot of people were looking at us.

'So how was your TEMPERATURE, Holly?' they will say *if* I get to school tomorrow.

'Oh, **very bad,** miss,' I'll say.

'Well, you didn't look too bad on the TV,' they'll say.

And then I'll have to say something like, 'Oh no, that was my scatty twin sister. I don't believe you've met her, miss . . . she left home in **DISGRACE**.'

I'm going to wear a disguise the next time we go racing.

Anyway, Dad, Grandpa and Sir Garfield took no notice of me telling them to use their indoor voices –

Fist Bump had **WON!**

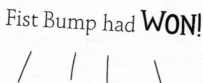

We didn't go home until after the last race. And then we stopped off at the Chequers until I said to Dad and Grandpa, 'Look, you MOOSES . . . if we don't get home before Mum we will *get it* in the neck . . . and she doesn't know I've got a temperature, if you remember.'

So we *just* got home before Mum; I changed quickly into my school clothes and dobbed Dad and Grandpa straight in it.

'I think they've been at the races,' I told Mum in a 'pretend-disapproving' voice.

'LOOK AT THE STATE OF YOU TWO.'

Mum said to Dad and Grandpa.

Dad said, 'Don't worry about that,' as he picked her up and gave her a big kiss – and then Dad and Grandpa started singing 'God Save the Queen' *again*.

And then Grandpa's phone rang and guess what? Lord Dorchester, the queen's Official Horse Trainer, wants to come and inspect High Five tomorrow! That is **OFFICIAL NEWS** – but it's also a secret.

GOD SAVE THE QUEEN – she may also save the Hopkinson family FINANCE department.

FUTURE NEWS

Pizza delivering is back off the menu, thank you very much.

CHAPTER 45

QUITE A LOT OF U-BEND STUFF

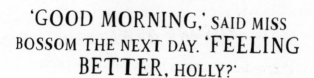

'GOOD MORNING,' SAID MISS BOSSOM THE NEXT DAY. **'FEELING BETTER,** HOLLY?'

'Better than what?' I asked – and then I remembered that I had a 'temperature' yesterday.

'Still feeling a bit poorly, Miss Bossom,' I added quickly in my 'FRAIL-AND-PALE' voice.

I had work to do spit-spot, in case you've forgotten, as I'd done a bit of a switcheroo with the play as Ed Shear'um is concerned.

'Look at my lovely pocket watch,' I said to Bossy Bottom while all the other kids were poking each other with things out in the playground.

'Yes, yes, Holly, it's very nice. I've seen it before, dear.'

So I gave her four verses of **SPIRO, SPERO** for being cheeky and patronising.

'Miss Bossom . . . we're not going to do your ridiculous *Cinderella* play, cos no one will buy tickets to it and the roof will fall in. We are going to do *School of Rock* and Ed Shear'um is going to come and watch, so we'll sell squillions of tickets.'

I was having to GABBLE a bit because this was no time for Felicity Slippery Snoop to be interrupting me – I *had* to get this one right!

'And you, Miss Bossom,' I continued, 'shall play the failed rock star who pretends to be the substitute teacher.'

'Oh yes, the lead role,' she said, her eyes misting over with excitement.

'And Felicity Snoop is going to play the miserable girlfriend who no one likes . . .'

'A perfect role for her.'

'And Daffodil needs a singing part.'

'Of course.'

My **MAGIC POCKET WATCH** and I are back in the game double-whopper time.

SEND MY REGARDS TO BROADWAY, HELLO, LEICESTER SQUARE.

So after break Miss Bossom clapped her hands and told everyone to pipe down.

'Now, children, I have *big news* this morning about our dramatic masterpiece,' she declared. 'We're going to switch our school play from *Cinderella and her Wicked Sisters* to *School of Rock*.'

Everyone in the class except Felicity Snoop gave a loud cheer.

'IT WAS HOLLY HOPKINSON'S IDEA, AND A BRILLIANT ONE.'

she went on.

Everyone turned and smiled at me.

'Nice one, Holly,' said Gaspar.

SUCCESS: I'm a hit at school!

Then Botty Bossom gave out the parts. But she's no fool – so guess which part she announced first, as if it was the greatest part ever?

The ocean-going gob-smackingly ghastly girlfriend . . .

'Felicity will play the girlfriend,' Botty said. I turned away in case Felicity caught me smirking, but to my amazement she looked like she'd won the lottery. I guess she doesn't care that the character is horrible – just that she has a big part.

Everyone else thought they had cool parts and then, like it was an afterthought, Miss Bossom said, 'Oh, and I shall help out by playing the naughty teacher.'

Then Bossy got a bit carried away and ONLY TOLD THE WHOLE CLASS that Ed Shear'um is definitely going to come and watch.

I did not say he was *definitely* coming. Now I'm under big pressure,

thank you

very much.

CELEBRITY NEWS – Vinnie has informed me that all the big farmers in the old days had names like Shear'um; so Ed has probably got a lot of sheep as well as records.

We got down to rehearsals right away. Daffodil is playing the shy girl who sings like an angel – and Vinnie's playing another shy kid who turns out to be a great guitarist. I'm the producer, which is fine, because I've already had a good helping of GLORY due to the change of play. And Brian sings a bit like his father at the races.

My legs had never felt happier on my way home; they skipped along and my fingers clicked as if I was a spring foal double-whopper FIZZING around the field.

BAND NEWS –

Harold and Stickly have *officially* engaged Harmony as their lyrics writer.

I think they should have asked Holly Hopkinson (BAND MANAGER INC) first, quite frankly. But that is musicians for you – they are very erroneous*.

Then Grandpa announced **TWO BIG BITS OF NEWS** – so big he got all the family into the kitchen as soon as Mum got back from her London compute:

* ERRONEOUS –
mistakenly over-excited.

Lord Dorchester fell in **LOVE** with High Five and said the queen would be delighted to give him a new home – and paid Grandpa a small fortune for him.

(BEANSTALK IS FURIOUS ABOUT THIS. ABSOLUTELY FURIOUS.)

Dad and Grandpa have only gone and bought the Chequers; they're going to turn it into a bristo pub**.

IT LOOKS LIKE THE HOPKINSONS ARE GOING TO BE **BIG CHEESES** IN LOWER GORING. FAREWELL, FINANCIAL MISERY.

PS Vera did something very un-Vera-like – she made a public declaration that Grandpa had been clever and brave to buy High Five – and that she had been wrong to **DOUBT** him.

** BRISTO PUB – a pub named after a square in Edinburgh apparently. I think Dad may need to rethink that one – no one wants to eat Scottish food – not even Scottish people.

CHAPTER 46

ROLL UP, ROLL UP

TODAY I AM UNDER MASSIVE PRESSURE – IT'S FINALLY THE DAY OF
THE SCHOOL PLAY.

But that doesn't mean that I can desert my duty as a writer – after all, Samuel Pepys didn't walk off the job when the flames were lapping around his feet and London was burning.

Ticket sales for this evening's Christmas show have gone through the roof (not literally, thank goodness).

(TICKETS)

Thanks in no small part to the rumour about *School of Rock*, but also because Daffodil has been going around telling everyone that a top-secret VIP celebrity singing guest is coming.

Sometimes I think I should think through my plans a bit more; with hindsight I might have realised that doing *School of Rock* could go *horribly* wrong.

We could all be heading for proper, double-whopper helpings of stuff you don't even want to think about if the play totally fails, and singer, songwriter and farmer Ed Shear'um doesn't turn up.

I couldn't even begin to finish my breakfast. What I had forgotten is that I need the *audience* to think the show is great, not just me.

When it was 'show time', as we say in the business, everyone was pouring into the school hall, soaking wet as it was lashing down with rain. And the rainwater was pouring down the inside of the walls as well!

Literally everyone was turning up – except Aleeshaa, who **wasn't** invited – thank you very much.

Mrs Smartside (Chairman of School Governors) arrived with the vicar – and they sat smack in the middle of the front row.

Slinky Dave was 'on the door' WITH STRICT INSTRUCTIONS:

NO TICKET. ADIOS. MON AMI.

(AS THEY SAY IN SICILY).

And strictly **no** exceptions; apart from:

1. Ed Shear'um.

2. Any celebrities who happen to be in the area and *not* busy buying burgers and fizzy drinks in Chipping Topley.

Then I realised I was wrong. *Everyone* was *not* in the hall. At that particular moment Grandpa and Vinnie had less presence than Banksy.

In other words, they were nowhere to be seen.
They had vanished into thin air –

VAMOOSED!

Not only that, but Ed was showing no sign of
turning up, either.

I looked at the rain coming in through the leaky
roof and suddenly, I knew *exactly* where *they* were.

And probably where
Ed Shear'um was too.

CHAPTER 47

DICK TURPIN-RY

I WAS **DOUBLE-WHOPPER** SOAKED
BY THE TIME I GOT TO THE EDGE OF THE
VILLAGE WHERE GRANDPA AND HIS NEARLY
SILENT SIDEKICK WERE IN THE PROCESS OF
TRAPPING THE NEXT UNFORTUNATE SOUL
TO DRIVE INTO THEIR **WATER TRAP** -
AND THAT PERSON WAS GOING TO BE
ROYALLY 'NOT AMUSED',
THANK YOU VERY MUCH.

I'd told Daffodil to make everyone hold fire on starting the show until I returned, but if Ed didn't *arrive de vederchi* the whole thing was going to be a washout, literally and un-literally.

Before I could say, 'Unplug that road, you two highwaymen,' guess what happened?

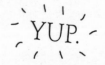

YUP.

The ginger singer came winging round the corner in a sports car, and slammed straight into Grandpa and Vinnie's handmade flood.

TITANIC WHOOSH.

Quite a lot of the splash went over me, thank you very much.

'Hello . . . it's the drummer's manager,' Ed chirped without a care in the world as he wound down his window. So I did a big curtsy – just in case celebrities like that sort of thing.

'Hello, Ed,' I said. 'Er . . . how are your sheep? Welcome to Lower Goring.'

'Sheep? What on arth are you on about . . . and what are you doing on the side of the road?' he wanted to know.

'Oh, just checking on some drummers and stuff,' I said. 'Actually, you never know where you're going to find them.'

'Well, I'm a bit stuck . . . and I'm going to be late for your play.'

'Oh, don't worry about *that*,' I said. '*They* are going to get you there on their tractor RIGHT NOW, FREE OF CHARGE,' (in my 'threatening' voice while stabbing my fingers in the general direction of my criminal so-called associates).

CHAPTER 48

RANK BEING PULLED

SLINKY DAVE WAS LOOKING A BIT **SHAKEN UP** ON THE DOOR.

'It's getting nasty in there with all this waiting for the show to begin,' he said. 'They're asking for their money back.'

And then Slinky Dave saw our world-famous pop star and snapped to attention.

'Steady on, Dave,' I whispered. 'He's incommune ocado *.'

* INCOMMUNE OCADO –
some place no one delivers to.

'I'll find you a good seat,' I advised Ed, sounding like I was in control. I could have a new star on my hands here. I might end up handling all his sheep and recordings stuff. 'Just hold on there for a second.'

Mrs Chichester had beaten Mum to the seat next to Mrs Smartside, so the front row was full.

But Mrs Smartside sprang into action as soon as she saw my secret guest hovering around with his wild mop of hair. So she told the vicar to 'Hop it, pronto,' and make way for the mega-star.

Vera and soggy Grandpa (finally) sat down next to Dad two rows behind Mum.

Harold, Harmony and Stickly had even turned up and were texting in the back row next to Beanstalk and Barkley. Which was actually pretty handy as Wolfe's nerves got to him and he had a bad attack of the SQUITS. So as Harold's band manager, I volunteered him to step in.

CELEBRITY NEWS – You JUST WON'T believe it – as we were about to start,

Andrew LORD arrived.

'I hope you don't mind,' Andrew Lord said to Ms Growler, 'but I just happened to be passing and thought I'd drop in to see how it goes.' You just couldn't make it up! She didn't have a clue *what* he was talking about or why he was there.

Finally, after all that TURBULATION, Daffodil gave me the nod. It was

SHOW TIME!

And I stepped out of the wings on to the stage . . .

'Welcome to our school play,' I said to the audience. 'As many of you already know, Cinderella is for losers. Prince Charming is yesterday's news.

Today, you are at

THE SCHOOL OF ROCK.'

And this is the clever bit – as I said that, Daffodil ran on to the stage and ripped down the *Cinderella and her Wicked Sisters* banner – under which was the *School of Rock* sign. Then Harold gave me a cheeky wink and hit the drums like a born performer, and Vinnie struck a few chords as Miss Bossom came flying on to the stage via our homemade slide.

The next few seconds were pivotal.*

Mum's mouth fell open as if she was watching a vision of the future in which the ladies-in-waiting were having a scrap with the gardeners over the last egg-mayonnaise sandwich at her garden party.

314

* PIVOTAL – just getting to the bog in time when you're bursting.

 ← Mrs Chichester, sulking at the back, looked like someone had taken their builder into her shop.

Mrs Smartside looked like someone had parked a load of ROTTEN kippers under her nose for a few weeks. →

BUT:

Ed Shear'um leaped to his feet and shouted, 'Rock 'n' roll, baby!' and the rest of the hall went mental!

Harmony and Stickly got totally carried away air-guitaring along to Vinnie's riffs, and Aunt Electra, late as usual, showed up in the nick of time to do some bohemian WAGGLING. Even Vera did some nodding with her head.

Miss Bossom knocked it out of the park (I'm thinking of signing her up too just in case she gives up this teaching lark). And all of the kids were awesome. I even have to admit that Felicity Snoop isn't terrible at playing an awful girlfriend.

By the time we'd all taken our bows and the final curtain dropped, the crowd were all on their feet giving it large. Even Ms Growler stood up and began to clap her hands out of time.

Then, backstage, Daffodil, Vinnie and I had a BOGEY-CLUB huddle.

'WE **DID IT**, GUYS,' I said.

'YORKEL,' agreed Vinnie.

'NICE BIT OF BREAKFAST,'

added Daffodil, not forgetting to deploy her finger.

AND ENOUGH TICKETS WERE SOLD TO PAY FOR A NEW FLIPPING ROOF.

Finally, Mum and Dad came and gave me a cuddle and told me I was a very clever girl, which was quite pleasing for Holly Hopkinson

(YOUNGEST OF THE FAMILY).

And Harmony sidled up to me and gave me a sort of sideways, one-armed hug. 'You know, you're not so AWFUL at this stuff, little sis,' she said. Then she winked at Harold. '*You* were rubbish, though, of course.'

'Whateva!' said Harold, but he was kind of laughing.

But the *best* bit was when we all went over the road to the Chequers to celebrate with mountains of fish fingers and ice cream with a cheeky dash of curry powder added. (That is going to be big in the culinary world one day – you heard it here first.) Although Beanstalk turned her nose up at that new dish.

And the Hopkinson family had a very embarrassing group hug – but it was kind of nice.

THANK YOU, **MAGIC POCKET WATCH**.

This is officially the best day of Holly Hopkinson's life – ever.

I HAVE OFFICIALLY SURVIVED BEING KIDNAPPED TO THE COUNTRYSIDE BY MY PARENTS. AND YOU KNOW WHAT . . . MAYBE, JUST MAYBE IT ISN'T SO BAD, AFTER ALL.

THE END

(OF HOLLY HOPKINSON'S MEMOIRS VOLUME I.

WHICH ARE NOW GOING INTO A TIME CAPSULE TO BE HIDDEN SOMEWHERE IN GRANDPA'S FARMYARD WHERE HAROLD AND HARMONY WON'T GET THEIR PRYING MITTS ON THEM).

Thank you very much.

EPILOGUE

ANNUAL REPORT OF HOLLY HOPKINSON GROUP OF COMPANIES

I CAN REPORT THAT

HOLLY HOPKINSON
(BAND MANAGER INC)

NOW HAS FULL CONTROL OF THE BAND (NO NAME YET – WHICH IS DELAYING REHEARSALS – TOP OF TO-DO LIST) AS HARMONY HAS SIGNED UP TOO. IT WILL BE IN NEGOTIATION WITH THE CHEQUERS TO HAVE FIRST DIBS ON ALL LIVE MUSIC GIGS. I HAVE ASSURED THE MANAGEMENT THAT HAROLD WON'T FREEZE ON STAGE AGAIN. AND I'M WAITING FOR A REPLY FROM ED SHEAR'UM.

322

It's a good job that Harold is finally going to be a rock star because his school report has come in and it isn't good. Though when Mum and Dad tried to talk to him about it he just GRUNTED. Harold seems to think that making noises normally associated with bison and trapped wind is a reasonable way to communicate.

Grandpa has officially signed up to partnership on all activities that involve horseracing – the recently formed

HOLLY HOPKINSON
(RACING ASSOCIATE)

will get a ten per cent cut.

Grandpa and Vinnie have signed a PR deal with HOLLY HOPKINSON PR INC to keep them *out* of the press (as it turns out, PR people get you out of the media as well as in it).

So, in other words, HH PR INC has promised not to tell RoundaboutChippingTopley.com and the *Daily Chipping Topley Mail* what Grandpa/Vinnie do when it rains.

Talks have also started with Dad to see if HH PR INC can tell some foodie writers what to write.

Exploratory discussions with Mum have started to see if *my* people can talk to *her* people. I'm thinking we could bring her up to speed on some of these books she doesn't read for book club – or at least make sure that book club doesn't find out that she **doesn't** read any of them.

My people will tell *her* people that it's better to be proactive* than reactive.**

Things are **great** with my official countryside best friend, Daffodil, and if Vinnie plays his cards right, he is in with a shout of getting upgraded too.

So, to conclude this volume for the second time, I think it is fair to say that our move to the countryside has **not** been as **DISASTROUS** as many thought it might be.

And unbelievably there is ***LAST-MINUTE NEWS*** from Aleeshaa – she has **found** her lost phone and seen all the messages she has missed – and is going to come and stay soon.

---

* PROACTIVE – better hourly rate for holiday jobs.

** REACTIVE – having to tell porkies.

PS According to the people from the Amazon, my smartphone is en croute.*** YES, FINALLY MY PARENTS HAVE HAD THE SENSE TO EQUIP ME LIKE A NORMAL HUMAN BEING, THANK YOU VERY MUCH. So my business empire will be **FLOURISHING** soon.

*** EN CROUTE –
wrapped up and on its way.

LITERALLY THE FINAL, FINAL NEWS

So I was lie-ing in bed* last night thinking that everyone was asleep, and just finishing off this volume of my memoirs when guess what happened?

YES.

I started to hear this tapping from the attic. Quite gentle to start with, but definitely not the heating pipes which don't work.

So I shouted, 'Actually *not* funny, Harold and Harmony . . . go away . . . I know it's you . . . not Mabel.'

Then a few minutes later the tapping started again – so I decided to give Harold some of his own medicine. I put a sheet over my head and tiptoed down to his bedroom.

I could see he was pretending to be asleep in bed so I leaped on top of him, making SPOOKY noises.

326

* LIE-ING IN BED – having dreams which aren't true.

And he hit the roof screaming his head off – he really had been asleep.

So who was making the flipping tap, tap, tap noises up in the attic, excuse you?